THE MERRIMENT KIDS ADVENTURES

THE MERRIMENT KIDS ADVENTURES

By
Don L.
Bakke

**Illustrations by
Natasha Hill**

Published by Fast Dog Press
www.fastdogpress.com

Book design by Fast Dog Press
Illustrations by Natasha Hill

ISBN: 978-0-9840413-7-4

First Edition
05 04 03 02 01 11 12 13 14 15

Publisher's Cataloging-in-Publication available upon request

Don Bakke
Email: domabak@comcast.net

Chapter One

Our story begins in the small village of Merriment located on a hillside next to a vast forest and our story takes place in a time before cell phones, iPads and drones existed. Our story begins now . . .

Merriment villagers always looked forward to the holiday season as their favorite time of the year...most of all...the children. Especially, the children from Miss Dubbin's 4th grade class. You see, each year the 4th grade class has the honor of finding the "perfect" tree for the village square.

"O.K. class", shouted Miss Dubbin. "Is everybody ready for the great Merriment tree hunt?"

Nothing more needed to be said. The room was a swirl of children looking for scarves, boots, hats, coats, lunch bags, and everything needed to keep them warm on this much anticipated tradition. Out the door the

"Christmas tree finders" went. The group was comprised of three 4th graders - Becca, Billy and Freddy; one 3rd grader - Stephie, who would miss this event next year because her family was moving; one 5th grader - Thaddeus, who missed last year because of illness; and one dog named Scooter, who would be the official mascot. These students, plus teacher Miss Dubbin, made a total of six people in the party.

Out the door the Merriment tree hunters went. They would take turns leading each other into the woods with the teacher following behind to make sure there were always five in the party. The children agreed to let Becca be the first leader and Stephie the second. Miss

Dubbin thought the boys displayed good manners by letting the girls go first. The truth be known...the boys liked the idea of the girls guiding in the more familiar woods, while the boys being the skilled woodsmen they felt they were, would guide them in the less known woods. Little did they know that the group would be in "less known woods" almost from the start.

Becca had decided to choose the path that started from behind the old blacksmith's shop. None of the children had ever been on this path before because they had always been told to stay away from the horses for fear of being kicked. On this particular day the blacksmith had gone out of town to return a line of horses to a rancher not far away. Becca, being the first leader, decided it would be a good chance to see that part of the woods. The boys didn't seem real excited about exploring this different part of the forest. Somehow the trees looked older and larger and everything a bit darker. But, if Becca decided on that path, the boys weren't going to let her know they might be afraid. Having only come to the village of Merriment this past fall, Miss Dubbin was the least familiar with any part of the woods. And Scooter? He was just happy to be along.

"Now class", Miss Dubbin said. "We better not venture too far into the woods. We wouldn't want to get lost."

"Oh don't worry about getting lost," little Freddy Rodriguez said. "We've all been in the woods before."

Deep down everybody in the class thought that everybody else knew more about the woods than they themselves did. And maybe they did...maybe.

The class had decided that each "leader" would guide the party about the same distance as that of the schoolhouse to the Merriment grocery store. They were all very familiar with that distance because the grocery store was the only source of candy in town.

"O.K. Becca," said Miss Dubbin. "You may begin leading our search party. Everybody stay close together."

For some reason Becca wasn't as anxious as before to take that first step into the woods. She turned around to look at the class. There was no way they offered encouragement. She knew she would have to begin or she would receive a lot of teasing. Besides, she is the one who had chosen this spot. It was too late now.

Off they went. First Becca Anderson, followed by Stephie Kim, followed by little Freddy Rodriguez, who was followed by big Billy Tons, followed by Thaddeus Smith followed by Miss Dubbin with the king of the Shih

Tzus, Scooter, the last member of the party to enter the woods.

The snow was not very deep in most places. Whenever they came to a little clearing amongst the trees the snow seemed to be a bit deeper. Miss Dubbin explained to the children how the huge trees would stop some of the snow from reaching the ground and how they shouldn't be fooled by how much snow they think might have fallen.

It wasn't very long before the children began to get tired. It seemed that the snow in the meadows was getting deeper the farther they walked into the woods. After Becca had led the party the agreed upon distance, she had given way to Stephie. When Stephie had about finished leading her turn, they came to another clearing. The teacher suggested that this would be a nice place to have their picnic lunch. Everybody was very happy with that idea having become tired, thirsty and very hungry. In fact, Miss Dubbin could not remember seeing each child eat their OWN lunch so quickly. Usually, during the lunch hour, the kids were more interested in what the others had brought from home than what they themselves had brought. This usually ended in trades—peanut butter sandwiches for roast beef sandwiches—apples for oranges—cake for doughnuts and so on...but not this time. Everyone was thankful for whatever they found in their own lunch bags.

"Would anyone care for hot chocolate?" asked Miss Dubbin.

"Yes, yes, yes!!!" was the immediate response.

So the children topped off their lunches with steaming hot chocolate. Big Billy Tons looked a little sad.

"Is anything wrong, Billy?" asked Miss Dubbin.

"Oh, he's sad because we all finished our own lunches instead of him finishing them for us," said Thaddeus.

The children laughed.

"I don't think it's funny," exclaimed an amply proportioned Billy. "I could starve and blow away with the wind. Then what would you do when your parents put those sardine sandwiches and cups of broccoli in your lunch and tell you to finish everything because there are starving children in the world? You wouldn't have a starving child to give it to. You would have to eat it yourself!!"

The children stopped laughing. Billy had made sense.

"With no starving child to give it to, we'd have to eat it ourselves," agreed Becca.

"Yes. We know it would be a real waste to throw it away," noted Freddy Rodriguez.

"Well children. Maybe there is a lesson to be learned here," added Miss Dubbin. "Maybe we should have your parents pack a little less in your lunch…especially, if it's not your favorite for the day. If everyone took just a little less for themselves we might be able to break the all-time record for contributions to our food-shelf."

"Well, wait a minute…" Billy started to say.

"Ah, don't worry about it Billy. You'll still be taken care of," said little Freddy Rodriguez. "I would never deprive you of the peanut butter- tofu- broccoli sandwich my mother thinks is so wonderful."

Billy and all the children laughed. It was good to end their lunch on a high note.

Miss Dubbin was more serious now.

"I think we had better find our tree soon, boys and girls," she said. "It seems to be getting a bit windier all the time."

She really didn't have to tell them about the wind growing stronger. The kids had noticed the howling of the wind growing as it swept through the woods. It was in and out, over and under and in total control of the tree's flapping arms.

"This is starting to be like some monster stories my big brother told me," quivered Freddy.

"Yes. It sure is starting to get spooky," added Big Billy.

"I'm kind of scared," Stephie whimpered as she pulled her scarf up over her mouth and cheeks.

"Ah, come on," Becca shouted. "We came to find a tree for the town square and everyone's acting like it's Halloween!"

This didn't seem to help. The children were huddling closer and closer and shaking all the more.

"Children, I believe Becca is right," said Miss Dubbin. "We have to find a tree for the village square. Think of how proud the people of Merriment will be when they see us walking down Main Street with our 'tree of the year.' "

"Yes" an older Thaddeus agreed. "We have to find our tree!"

The tree brigade started to feel a little braver now. They quickly packed their lunch bags into their knap-sacks.

Chapter Two

Soon they were on their way with Freddy assuming complete control. Miss Dubbin was happy to see the children's eagerness return because deep down she was worried about the weather herself. She decided they had better pick a tree very soon and start heading back. All six people in the party seemed to be in complete agreement. Everyone was anxious to head back. They decided to choose their tree at that moment.

"Now remember class," said Miss Dubbin. "The tree we pick must be large enough so the whole village of merriment can see it in the square and yet small enough so we can drag it out of the woods."

The decision was going to be hard. With all the tree's arms waving up and down, they appeared to be almost human. Each one seemed to be trying to "out-do" the one next to it. They seemed to be pleading to be the special tree which would stand in the village and have the townspeople decorate it with all the festive trimmings.

"Class," suggested Miss Dubbin. "We should look for a group of trees that are so close together that they may have trouble growing larger. We will take the tree which is most beneficial to us and with its removal...most beneficial to the woods."

"Sure," said Stephie Kim. "It's like what we were talking about yesterday—about living things in the world. About sharing sunlight, water, space and many other things we do with our neighbors here and afar."

"AND FOOD!" Added Billy.

Everyone laughed.

"Yes," Miss Dubbin said. "We will pick the tree which when removed will give its surrounding trees more space, sunlight, water and..."

"AND FOOD!!" chimed the class.

"Yes," said Miss Dubbin..."those important nutrients in the soil."

After some discussion they decided upon a tree, which could have been the "grandfather" of all the surrounding trees. Or the "grandmother" as Stephie put it. Miss Dubbin was concerned about being able to get the tree back to the village because of its size. The children felt the six of them - if Miss Dubbin would care to help - would be able to pull it back to Merriment. The class had brought along a "two-man" saw, or "two-people" saw as Becca put it, instead of an ax. They knew that safety was always a first consideration on their field trips. An ax was just a bit more dangerous to handle. They decided they could have three teams of two - if Miss Dubbin would care to help - to take turns sawing down the tree. Miss Dubbin thought it funny how polite each two-some was while sawing. It hardly seemed they had started when they would voluntarily turn it over to the next "two-some." Miss Dubbin and Thaddeus sawed a little longer than the others. She knew they would have to or it would be some time before they would be heading back. Thaddeus didn't know what she was thinking but he wasn't going to quit before she did.

After some time, the kids were beginning to feel they had picked the wrong tree. A smaller tree would have taken less time to get down and they could be on their way. Yet, they wanted their tree to be the grandest tree to ever light up the town-square of Merriment.

The saw had passed the halfway mark now and Miss Dubbin estimated that if each two-some took "one more turn and really tried hard" the class and the tree would be on their way home. Becca and Stephie were the first two-some to accentuate their final turn with all the vim and vigor of two well-seasoned woodsmen...or "woods-persons" as Stephie quickly pointed out. Billy Tons and Freddy Rodriguez, next in line, were shocked to see Becca and Steph doing such a fine job on their last turn with the saw. When forming two-some's, Billy and Freddy wanted nothing to do with the girls. But, after seeing these "lumberjacks...er...lumber-Jills" work with such finesse, they began to have doubts about each other as partners. There was only one way to dismiss these uncertainties. When it came to be their final turn they would saw through the tree with all the determination of a "male-of-the-species" trying to loosen the "cap" of a bottle or jar which had just been handed to him by a " female-of-the-species."

It was now their final turn. Billy and Freddy grabbed the saw with all that fixed determination they had talked about. On a count of three they would let out all the pent-up emotions they had kindled for this final thrust to uphold their male dominance when it came to such matters.

"One," Billy counted.

"Two," Freddy counted.

"Three," they both counted.

S. H.

On the count of "three" they set upon the saw with a fury none of their classmates had ever seen before. At the very same time their feet dug into the snow to begin their charge, they both bounded forward as fast and as hard as they could. They forgot to decide who would go back and who would go forward. As a result, the saw stayed where it was and the boys bumped heads with almost the same ferocity as two mountain goats fighting for supremacy of their domicile. Almost the same...

"Billy! Freddy!! Are you all right?" A shocked Miss Dubbin asked.

"Dizzily speaking...I guess so," a dazed Billy responded.

"Dizzily speaking...I feel like I ran into the blacksmith's anvil," groaned Freddy.

After making sure there wasn't much more hurt than their pride, the class began to roar with laughter. Even Billy and Freddy had to laugh to think of how their antics had led to a "dizzy" trip into the snow-bank.

As everyone laughed, Miss Dubbin noticed that the wind was blowing harder and the flurries of snow were getting thicker. She knew they had to start back very soon. She asked Thaddeus if he would help her do the final bit of sawing. In a matter of minutes the tree was beginning to creak and about ready to fall down. No one was probably happier about this than the tree itself.

"Everybody get on the same side and help push the tree down," yelled Thaddeus.

The children huddled on the same side of the tree with Miss Dubbin and began pushing on the large trunk. Luckily, the class had made the cuts into the tree in just the right places. With little effort at all, the tree began to come down on its own.

"TIMBER!" yelled Freddy.

"TIMBER! TIMBER!" yelled the rest of the class.

And "TIMBER!" It did.

At first it started to fall slowly. And then it began to pick up speed until it hit the ground with a fully-grown "THWACK, THUMP, THUMPITY, THUMP, THWACK, THUMPITY, THUMP."

"Wow" was the unanimous yell roared by everyone as the tree finally lay quiet

Everyone began to explore the tree. Surely this would be the greatest tree to ever light up Merriment Square.

"Such a pretty tree!" an excited Stephanie yelled.

"Such a handsome tree!" an equally excited Freddy yelled. "Don't you agree Miss Dubbin?"

"Yes," Miss Dubbin replied. "It is a pretty handsome looking tree."

"Very dignified," declared Becca.

Even Scooter barked his approval.

It was a wonderful tree the class had selected. Once in Merriment, it would stand tall again with all the beautiful decorations the townspeople had worked so hard on through the fall.

Chapter Three

"O.K. class," instructed Miss Dubbin. "Let's have three people on each side of the tree evenly spread so we may begin preparing ourselves and the tree for our hike back home."

Immediately, the boys got to one side leaving the girls and Miss Dubbin on the other side.

While reaching into her bag, Miss Dubbin said, "Everyone take the rope from your knap-sack and tie it to a thick branch with the same kind of knot we worked on in the class-room.

The children began scurrying through their knap-sacks and bringing out the lengths of rope which had been supplied to them back home. In class they had learned to tie a "square-knot" around a yardstick preparing them for the time they would have to drag the tree out of the woods.

"Once your ropes are attached and ready to go, put your knap-sacks back on and stand ready to leave," Miss Dubbin ordered.

Miss Dubbin was getting nervous. The snow was falling harder to form an ever-thickening blanket of snow.

"Everyone ready?" Miss Dubbin asserted. "Grab hold of your ropes and we'll begin."

After a shaky start, the class had the tree moving smoothly down the path. Miss Dubbin and Thaddeus set a pretty fast pace knowing that if the snow kept falling at the rate it had been, their footing would become more difficult and slow them down. They had walked about twenty minutes when Miss Dubbin had them stop.

"Take a couple minutes to rest, children," said Miss Dubbin. "Thaddeus, will you come with me?"

Remembering that "hind-sight" is "twenty-twenty", Miss Dubbin now realized she should not have assumed the children knew everything about the woods they had gone into. Everyone thought it would be easy to walk out of the woods---just follow the path through the beautiful trees and meadows until the old blacksmith shop came into view. But, Miss Dubbin was noticing it to be more difficult than anticipated.

"Thaddeus," said Miss Dubbin when the two of them were a few yards away from the rest of the class. "I don't want to alarm you, but I'm not sure of where we are. I thought we would find our way back easily by following the path which had our footprints. But, now they have been covered by snow and all the different pathways look alike to me. Do you know where we are, Thaddeus?"

Thaddeus did not want to alarm Miss Dubbin.

"I'm not sure where we are either," he said. "But, I think we could find the right direction by using the sun."

Thaddeus was the only one in this group who knew a little about using the sun as a reference point to find which direction a person may be going. He remembered how his father and older brother John, who was a boy scout, would talk about how the sun rose in the East and set in the West.

"Not much sun to work with," commented Miss Dubbin. "We'll have to look for the brightest glare in the sky."

"What time is it, Miss Dubbin?" Thaddeus asked.

"Ten-thirty," she replied.

"Well, if it's 10:30, the sun must still be more East than West," Thaddeus thought out loud. "Wouldn't you agree, Miss Dubbin?"

"Yes, that makes sense," she agreed while looking for the brightest glare in the sky.

"I remember when we left the village and began walking into the woods, I could see the sun sneaking through the trees off my right shoulder," he pondered. "Now if the sun was rising..."

"Yes," Miss Dubbin jumped in. "And it's still rising because it's morning."

"Right," continued Thaddeus. "The sun should be on our left shoulder because we now want to walk in the opposite direction."

They both adjusted themselves as if the sun were a big yellow balloon floating high in the sky just off their left shoulders. Well...where they imagined that big yellow balloon would be anyway. It was still very gray with snowflakes filling the air.

“Now if our calculations are correct, Dr. Einstein,” Miss Dubbin said with a nervous smile. “We should be facing south, the direction we must head in order to get home.”

“That seems right, Miss Dubbin,” a smiling Thaddeus answered. “I know for a fact the black-smiths shop is in the north end of town facing the town-square. And being as we walked straight into the woods from behind the shop, we must have been going north…I hope.”

“We both hope,” Miss Dubbin uttered.

She hoped more than Thaddeus could ever imagine.

“O.K. ladies and gentlemen…Thaddeus and I have plotted our new course. Everybody back to their positions and we’ll be on our way,” Miss Dubbin said adding. “It’s going to take longer with the tree and the additional snow so let’s get moving!”

The children were not excited to resume the journey but somehow each of them could sense certain urgency in Miss Dubbin’s voice. They also noticed the snowfall becoming heavier and thus making it hard to drag the tree. But, they were determined to get the tree back to the townspeople. They worked together… each student moving as swiftly as he or she could while still moving as a unit. They walked for a considerable distance before Miss Dubbin told them they could take another break. It was a welcomed relief for all of them. Billy Tons said it seemed like they had walked for miles. The entire group agreed with him. Miss Dubbin knew they had not walked as far as it seemed.

"Class. I don't have to tell you that it isn't as pleasant a day as it had started out to be," Miss Dubbin stated. "I did not anticipate this kind of weather could come upon us so fast without warning."

"Here in the mountains it's not uncommon to have a quick change in the weather conditions," Freddy said. "These storms come up quickly and unannounced."

"Yes. One day we planned a picnic in the month of May and had to postpone it because of a snow-storm," added Stephanie.

Miss Dubbin, never having spent a winter in the mountains before, wished she had known how common these "unannounced" snowstorms were. She hoped they would see some "unannounced" sun pretty soon because it was becoming very hard to see through the ever thickening clouds overhead.

"Most of the time we welcome a surprise in the weather," Becca said.

"Yeah...but not now!" said Billy. "My feet and hands are cold. My boots are wet and I feel faint from lack of food."

The children didn't laugh at Billy like they might have at home. They were beginning to feel pretty hungry themselves.

"Miss Dubbin!" Thaddeus yelled. "It's becoming almost impossible to tell where the sun is in the sky."

"You're right," replied Miss Dubbin. "We better continue while we can faintly see where it should be in the sky. And children...I have been giving some thought to leaving the tree behind so we can make better time."

Tired, as they were, the children thought it too grand of a tree to be deserted now.

"Please, Miss Dubbin," Stephie pleaded. "Not now!"

"Not yet, anyway," Becca added.

"Please let us keep it a little longer," Freddy begged. "Let us keep it a little longer. We can make it."

"I'm not really fainting, yet," Billy said in a brave voice.

"I'm kind of proud of this tree myself," Thaddeus said. "It's a bigger and better tree than my class-mates brought back last year. I would sure like to see the looks on their faces when we come into town with this one."

Miss Dubbin was proud of the tree herself and knew that Thaddeus had taken some teasing from his peers for wanting to go with the "little fourth graders". But, she also had to consider the tree was endangering their progress to reach home.

"O.K. class," she decided. "We'll bring it with us a little longer. But, if the time comes when I think we should discard it, that's what we will do."

The children were happy with her decision and made ready to continue their journey. Everyone in the party was becoming more determined with each step. Getting the tree to the Merriment square was much more important to them than it would be to their parents in the same situation. They knew if their parents were with them, the tree would be left behind immediately. But, considering the time and effort that had gone into this splendid tree…it just didn't seem fair. Besides… they had their pride too. They didn't want to be the first fourth grade class to end up without a tree since the tradition began many years ago.

To the children, their reasoning was sound. But to Miss Dubbin, their reasoning was impractical. She knew her first consideration was for the safety of her group. She would give them a little bit longer with the tree...but, not much longer.

Chapter Four

"I think I see a meadow up ahead," Miss Dubbin yelled. "We'll have to hurry to the other side!"

Miss Dubbin was hoping to see a sign that would indicate they had been on this trail before ...but none was evident.

The tree was becoming harder to pull as the class tugged it farther into the meadow. The snow had been deeper in the meadows from the onset of their trip and now because of the fresh fallen snow, was becoming even more difficult to get through with the children sinking to their thighs.

Above the noise of the blowing wind and snow, Miss Dubbin shouted, "Children. We must leave the tree here!!!"

The children realized that the time had come to worry more about their own survival.

“Everyone form a line behind me and hold on to the person’s knap-sack in front of you so no one will get lost,” commanded Miss Dubbin.

The children, understanding the urgency of Miss Dubbin’s order, formed a column directly behind her. No one seemed concerned about who would be first or who would be last---it didn’t seem very important now. Their main concern was to finish crossing the meadow and hopefully to find a homeward bound path in the next stretch of woods.

Without having to pull the tree along, Miss Dubbin hoped the children would have more energy to force their bodies through the nearly knee-deep snow. She was also concerned about another element in the weather...wind-chill. The children had studied it in their weather unit and unknowingly were falling victim to it. Miss Dubbin could see how the cold air combined with the wind was turning the children’s faces to a deep red. If she didn’t find some protection soon, their cheeks might turn to ‘white’--- a sign of “frost-bite”.

“Class. Before we begin again,” she cautioned. “Those of you with scarves pull them over your face and leave them there. We must not have any exposed skin to the wind. Thaddeus, take my scarf.” Thaddeus didn’t argue. He had dressed a little lightly.

If the condition of the storm changed any...it was only for the worse.

"Remember," Miss Dubbin went on. "We must all be brave and strong. I know it's going to be hard for each of you to keep moving. But, it's going to be hard for all of us. Now hold on tight to the knapsack ahead of you and keep on moving."

There was not time for tears. The children did exactly as she ordered and began to move slowly forward. Scooter was hopping through the snow a few yards behind them. He also seemed sad to leave the tree behind.

It was now impossible for Miss Dubbin to see anything farther away than about two feet in front of her face. She knew she had to keep walking to get to the shelter of the woods on the other side of the meadow. Having taken about five steps since leaving the tree, Miss Dubbin felt a strange sensation. It was as if the ground below them was giving way. It was shaking as if they were experiencing an earthquake. THEN SHE SAW IT!!! A huge ravine opened in front of them. She realized now that they had walked out onto a ledge hanging over this "gorge" and turned to warn the children.

"CHILDREN!! TURN BACK!! HURRY!!!

It was too late. The ledge ripped away from the bank of this ravine and suddenly everyone was airborne tumbling head over heels to the bottom of this small canyon.

Snow was flying
And shoes and hats
No time for chits
And no time for chats
Children were flying
All good, no brats
Republicans followed by
Some democrats.
The tree came falling
Midst the final format
Including a bob-cat
Chased by a gnat.
A teacher, some mittens
A pitter and a pat
All were flying
Like circus acrobats.
Down the snow-covered canyon
With the snow made mat.
Jumping Jehosophat!
And that's about that!

There was silence for a few moments as everyone tried to remember where they were and what had happened. Miss Dubbin was the first to stir…gingerly. Something was wrong with her ankle. She didn't know if it was badly sprained or even worse—broken. She looked around and saw children and traces of children. She could see four heads and one set of legs sticking out of the snow. She called their names as they were wiping snow from their faces and everywhere else.

"Thaddeus?"
"Yes, Miss Dubbin," he answered.

"Becca?" she called.

"Yes, Miss Dubbin," she answered.

"Stephie and Freddy?" She called.

"Yes, Miss Dubbin," they answered.

"And Billy? " She called. "Where are you Billy?"

There was no answer. Only the stirring and pumping of the one set of legs sticking out of the snow. And if these legs could talk they were probably yelling..." GET ME OUT OF THIS MESS!!" At any rate, the class came to Billy's rescue. They grabbed a hold on each of his legs and pulled and tugged and tugged and pulled. They could see his belt-buckle. Again they pulled and tugged and tugged and pulled. They could see his scarf. Finally with a last pull and a last tug and a last tug and a last pull, they were able to see a completely un-covered Billy Tons.

"Whew! I didn't think you would ever find me," Billy panted from a shortness of breath. "It's a lonely world down there. Now I know what it's like to be one of the first snowflakes to fall to the ground and then be quickly covered by all the other snowflakes. It just doesn't seem fair."

"Oh well. In the springtime you "first" snowflakes are usually the last to melt," Becca said adding dramatically. "First to the ground and last to melt, a snowflakes life is not often felt."

The whole class roared with laughter and gathered around Billy to help him brush off the remaining snow.

Miss Dubbin was happy to see that all the children were accounted for and full of spirit. Still, some one was missing...Scooter. It was Scooter! Where could he be? She was afraid to guess. As small as he was, the avalanche of snow could have easily covered him. There was no telling where he might be. Miss Dubbin knew the children would soon discover him missing and decided, for their safety, she would have to tell an untruth---A LIE! Miss Dubbin firmly believed that to tell a lie was one of the worst things a person could do to another person. But, she also knew that time was of the essence and an exception had to be made. This party of people needed to use all their energy to secure their safety.

Becca was the first to notice and began looking around. She whistled—then called. "Scooter! Scooter! Where are you Scooter?"

Immediately, the rest of the class realized he was missing and joined in the search.

"Scooter! Here Scooter!" they yelled.
"Come on, boy! Here Scooter!
"Come on Scooter! Where are you buddy?"

More whistling and hollering followed. Miss Dubbin called for the boys and girls to listen to her but they had gone in different directions and were yelling quite loudly. All of a sudden the earth began to shake again and down the ravine about a hundred yards another snow-slide could be seen. Everyone became very quiet and slowly moved back to where Miss Dubbin was sitting.

"Children," Miss Dubbin said softly. "I tried to tell you. Scooter isn't here. I saw him run just before the rest of us began tumbling into the ravine. He seemed to sense what was going to happen and ran off barking as if he was going for help."

“That sounds like Scooter, “Freddy said.

“Yes. If anyone can find home, he will,” added Thaddeus.

“I hope he leads our parents to us,” sniffled Stephie.

“He will,” a confident Becca said. “And I hope they bring plenty of food and water.”

“Hey! Billy’s supposed to say that!” Freddy said with a wry smile.

“Yea. I’m supposed to say that!” agreed Billy.

“Well…go ahead and say it,” Becca conceded.

“O.K., I will!” Billy answered. “I hope they bring plenty of food AND HOT CHOCOLATE!!!!!”

“Yeeeeeaaaaahhh and Yaaaahooooo!!” all the children chimed. “Everything is back to normal!!!”

If only everything was back to normal, thought Miss Dubbin. For reasons of safety, she was happy the children were convinced that Scooter was on his way back for help. With no food and hardly any water, it would have been dangerous to let the children spend their energy digging through the snow looking for him. Every bit of their energy had to be directed toward survival and nothing else!!

JUST THEN! There was another roar a little farther down the ravine. The children huddled around Miss Dubbin.

"We can't stay down here any longer," warned Miss Dubbin. "There's too much danger of another snow-slide all around us."

"So who wants to stay and how do we get out?" Freddy asked nervously.

"The sides of the gorge are almost straight up and down," Thaddeus observed.

"I want my mommy," Stephie cried.

"We'll be ok, Steph," comforted Billy. "As soon as we get out of here."

Miss Dubbin knew the sides of the chasm were quite steep. But, they were the only way out. They could walk down the canyon floor to find another easier way out but they would also be taking a chance on another avalanche. At least where they were, the snow had already caved in…once.

"If we have to stay the night, at least we'll have some fire-wood," Becca said while gazing at the tree.

"For sure," Freddy grumbled. "If it wasn't for that tree we wouldn't be in this mess!"

The children seemed to agree with Freddy.

"Now let's not put the blame where it doesn't belong," Miss Dubbin said firmly. "We were wrong to go into a part of the woods we were not familiar with. And we were wrong by not paying closer attention to the weather conditions. AND we are wrong now to worry about what we should have done. Let's worry about what we are going to do!"

She need not say another word. The children understood. Everyone was now staring at the tree.

"I sure wish that tree was a ladder," Billy sighed as he daydreamed.

"I sure wish that tree was a ladder," mimicked Becca.

And then after a short pause….

“Hey! Wait a minute. Billy may have a way out of here!” She said excitedly.

“I may? I mean…I might? I mean, I do?” a confused Billy uttered.

Thaddeus was the first to glance from the tree to the top of the embankment and back to the tree again.

“It might just work! “He shouted.

“What might just work?” asked Miss Dubbin.

“Billy thought of using the tree as a ladder,” answered Becca.

“I did? I mean…I what? I mean…I DID!!” Billy finally realized.

“If we set it on end, the tree should be tall enough to enable us to climb out of here,” Thaddeus explained.

“I like the way you people think,” a positive Miss Dubbin said. “Let’s give it a try!”

As Miss Dubbin began to stand, the class could see in her face she was in a lot of pain.

"Miss Dubbin! Something's wrong! Did you hurt yourself?" Becca asked while helping her teacher to her feet.

"It's my ankle," Miss Dubbin said while grimacing. "I seemed to have sprained it in the fall off the ledge."

Miss Dubbin explained to the class that the one good thing about all the snow was that she was able to pack it around her ankle to keep the swelling down. She said that though it hurt, she could still move it and that's what she planned on doing.

"Now, let's get on with it," she ordered.

Billy was daydreaming some more.

"If we had a rope it might be easier for the people on top to support the tree while those left down below climb up," he thought.

"Anyone in particular you're worried about?" Freddy giggled.

"Billy does have a good idea," Miss Dubbin interjected. "With someone on top holding the tree steady, there would be less chance of it sliding to either side."

"But, we don't have a rope," Becca countered.

"Yes, we do," Billy answered as he pointed to the tree. "We can untie our individual ropes from the tree and tie them together to form one long rope."

"The fellow is brilliant," Freddy exclaimed.

"Great idea, Billy," Miss Dubbin added.

"It's kind of fun to think of something other than food," Billy said proudly.

The class laughed.

"O.K., let's get this tree in the proper position," Miss Dubbin requested.

The class removed their ropes and then aligned themselves along the tree. Thaddeus, Billy and Miss Dubbin were towards the end of the tree that would be the top. They were a little taller and would have more leverage when pushing the tree up right

"On the count of three give it the old heave-ho," Miss Dubbin said with an encouraging voice.

"I wish on a count of three, it was 'presto' and I was back home sitting next to a fireplace in my long woolies!" Freddy mumbled.

"Here we go, "Miss Dubbin commanded. " One…"

"Let's make it good," added Thaddeus.

"Two…"

"No argument here," Becca responded.

"Thrreeee!!!"

At that moment the whole class was energized together and able to get the top of the tree moving upward to the edge of the ravine. Everybody was excited.

"It's working," Billy yelled.

"Don't let go," Miss Dubbin ordered.

All the kids were yelling encouragement to anyone who would listen.

"Keep pushing!" ---"It's just about there!"---"Steady! Keep it steady!"—"Pretty soon we can go home!!! ---"It's looking good!"

The tree had lined up against the wall of the ravine as good as or even better than the class anticipated.

“A stair-way to the stars,” Freddy said dramatically.

“I hope it’s a stairway home to some hot soup,” responded Thaddeus.

“And my mommy and my daddy,” Stephie added tearfully.

“Well, let’s give it a try,” Becca suggested.

“Right you are, Bec,” Miss Dubbin agreed. “Let’s get moving. Thaddeus...You go first.
You’re the oldest and strongest and can help the others climb onto the top of the ledge once you’re up there. I’ll remain down here and be the last one up in order to steady the base of the tree for the rest of you.”

The class could see that Miss Dubbin was in a lot of pain from her ankle sprain and that she might not be able to climb up the tree without some help from down below. There was a brief pause...and then Billy volunteered saying, “Well, being it was my idea, I want to take some responsibility to make sure it’s successful.”

"What do you mean?" asked Miss Dubbin.

"I'll be the last one up," Billy answered. "Besides...we need everyone up on top to help me over the ledge."

"Yes. And Billy should be able to keep the base of the tree real steady by leaning against it," Freddy said half-kidding.

"How about if I lean against you first?" Billy threatened.

"Billy! Freddy! Stop that bickering!!" Miss Dubbin scolded. "We don't have time for that! Thank you for volunteering. You can stay down with me. I know you'll do a very good job, Billy. You're very strong. O.K....Thaddeus. Let's go for it!"

Thaddeus was a very good choice to be the first to climb up the wall of the small canyon. As was the case of most children in Merriment, Thaddeus was an avid tree-climber and had developed many skills in that area. Thaddeus's weight helped to sink the tree into the snow a little bit and that helped stabilize it even more. He was making good progress. Limb by limb he climbed toward the top of the tree. His progress began to slow a little when he neared the top because the limbs grew thinner and more limber and therefore began to bend more as he stepped on them.

"About three more branches and he should be up, "Freddy said with his fingers crossed for good luck inside his mittens.

"Be careful," yelled Steph!
Just as Stephie yelled, Thaddeus slipped. Everyone screamed! Luckily, he was able to stop his fall by grabbing onto the limbs and regaining his footing.

"Are you ok?" Miss Dubbin yelled.

"I'm fine," Thaddeus called back.

"Maybe you should come down," Miss Dubbin suggested.

"No. No. I'll make it this time," Thaddeus assured her and the class.

Again, Thaddeus began to climb the upper half of the tree.

"I'm kind of nervous," Freddy said.

"I won't be able to make it," Stephie said tearfully.

"We're all going to make it," Miss Dubbin assured her. "Once Thaddeus gets on top we can use part of the rope to help the next climber up. We'll tie it around your waist and almost be able to pull you up."

Stephie smiled.

This time when Thaddeus was near the top three or four branches, he was a little more careful. He had not let on to the rest of the class the fear he felt when he lost his footing and slipped. The fear came not from the thought of falling to the snow (he had already done that and not been hurt) but from the thought of this being their only good chance of survival. If he didn't make it to the top…he doubted anyone else would either.

"Two more branches to go," Thaddeus thought to himself.

This time he didn't slip. He was careful not to lean too hard on the edge. He didn't want another avalanche…. especially with the class down below.

There was absolute silence. All attention was completely on Thaddeus. One more branch to go. Thaddeus was close. He was now able to swing one leg over to the top of the ledge. He was halfway. He had to be careful. He began to shift his weight from the tree to the ledge.

Luckily, they had chosen the right place to lean the tree against the wall of the ravine. They had chosen the exact spot everyone had fallen down from as a result of the cave-in. Therefore, all the overhanging snow had fallen with them and Thaddeus was stepping onto snow with a solid earth below it.

The time had come for Thaddeus to completely depart from the tree and land on the ledge. He sprang forward as far as he could while extending his arms and trying to grasp anything that would help him anchor into the snow.

"He did it!!" shouted Becca.

"He did it! He did it!!" everyone shrieked.

Thaddeus lay motionless for a moment to catch his breath and to be certain he was solidly entrenched.

"Phew! "He thought to himself. "Now to rescue the others."

He wrapped part of the rope around his waist and threw the rest over the side. Freddy would be the first to ascend the tree followed by Becca, Stephie, Billy and Miss Dubbin.

Freddy scaled the tree quite easily with the help of Thaddeus pulling on the rope. Becca almost flew up with both Thaddeus and Freddy helping her. Stephie was no problem. But, then came Billy Tons. Miss Dubbin insisted that he be next. Thaddeus decided it was time for them to take a short break to catch their breath. Billy knew what they were thinking and vowed to himself if he was able to get out of this "nightmare" he would certainly improve his physical condition. Yes sir…exercise and diet for Big Billy Tons.

"O.K. class," Miss Dubbin yelled from below. "Take a deep breath and get ready to help Billy up."

By now the class was standing four deep with a part of the rope in each of their hands. This would be harder than the "tug-of-war" they had with the 7th grade class.

"One, two, three, GO!" shouted Miss Dubbin.

At the signal Billy started climbing the tree. The class was pulling with all their might and Miss Dubbin was pushing from down below. Billy's legs were churning up the side of the tree like a buzz saw. He knew if he didn't make the first time he would be too tired to try a second time.

"He's making it!" shouted Thaddeus. "Keep pulling!"

Billy was making progress all right. His legs were a "blur ". The branches were flying; the people were puffing…everyone trying. He was nearing the top!!

"Just a few more feet," Thaddeus said encouragingly.

"Come on, Billy!" they all shouted. "You're just about here!!"

A few more broken branches and Billy made a lunge towards the class. He landed face down in the snow…but safe.

“We did it! He made it!” cheered his classmates.

Billy was happy but not excited.

“What’s wrong?” asked Becca.

“I don’t know if there are enough branches left for Miss Dubbin to climb up on,” answered Billy.

“Miss Dubbin! Time to get Miss Dubbin!” they all shouted as they looked back over the ledge.

They looked to the bottom of the ravine to see Miss Dubbin gazing into the sky with a thankful look on her face.

“We did it!” shouted Stephie.

“Yes, you did,” responded Miss Dubbin. “I’m very proud of you. That was quite a challenge.”

“It’s your turn!” hollered Billy.

"I'm not sure I can make it with my ankle feeling the way it does," Miss Dubbin replied.

"But, you have to try," Becca countered. "Remember your famous words? There is nothing wrong with failing a task if you have tried your very hardest."

"Thanks," Miss Dubbin remembered. "Those words of encouragement along with some very strong backs might get me out of here."

The kids threw down the rope and Miss Dubbin tied it around her waist like the others had done. She began to climb up. She was moving slower than Billy had—partly because of her sprained ankle and partly because there were few solid branches left to climb on. Nearing the top, the kids pulled her over the edge with ease. Everyone was ecstatic!

"We made it!" shouted Stephie.

"I can't believe it," Freddy said in disbelief.

"Wow," Billy said. "I thought we were 'goners."

"Well, were not out of it yet," Becca reminded everyone.

The class became quiet.

Chapter Five

“Yes. We still have some work to do,” Thaddeus added.

Grimacing in pain, Miss Dubbin said, “Yes class. You still have to find your way out of here.”

“You mean ‘WE’ still have to, “Billy said correcting her.

“No. I mean YOU,” Miss Dubbin said with authority. “I can’t seem to walk on my ankle. I would just slow you down.”

“But, Miss Dub…” the student’s voices trailed off as Miss Dubbin would hear no more of it.

“Thaddeus will be in charge and make any big decisions!” she said. “Stay close together and try to find a way around the ravine and then head in the same direction as before.”

“You could sit on the tree and we could pull you along,” pleaded Billy.

All the kids agreed.

"No!" Miss Dubbin said firmly. "It would take too much time and energy. There will be no arguing. Once you reach safety, you can send a rescue team for me."

"It's so hard to leave you behind," Stephie tearfully murmured.

"I know," Miss Dubbin said. "It won't be for long. I know you'll come back for me."

Miss Dubbin had to be brave. The safety of the children would be in more jeopardy if they were held back by her. The snow was falling and getting deeper, the wind was blowing harder than before, and it was getting colder. They had to go now.

Thaddeus and Billy pulled the tree up from the wall of the ravine.

"The tree will give you some shelter from the weather," said Thaddeus.

"We'll prop it alongside of you for protection," added Billy. "You might even want to use it as a blanket."

This was not a joyful thing for the children to have to do. No one wanted to leave their teacher behind.

"No more time," Miss Dubbin ordered. "Give me a hug and be on your way."

The children all hugged her and exchanged well wishes. They had grown to respect and care for one another through the predicament they shared.

Chapter Six

They were off. The bigger kids were leading in order to stomp down the snow to make easier footing for the smaller kids. Thaddeus was the first. He was followed by Billy, Becca, Stephie and Freddy. Stephie didn't want to be last. For that matter...neither did Freddy. Thaddeus had taken a stick to poke in the snow ahead of him if he wasn't sure of the footing. It would take a while to get around the ravine and headed in the direction of Merriment.

"Maybe we should have climbed up the other side of the gorge," Billy thought out loud.

"It was too high," Thaddeus explained. "We could never have reached the top."

On and on, the group moved on
Breaking through snow like newborn fawn.
They then formed a circle to catch their breath
Strategy was important...they could be facing death.
And then by fate or luck what have you

The entrance to a cave came into view.
The "fear-frozen" children couldn't believe their eyes
A chance for survival—there was joy in their cries.
They ran to the tunnel…cautiously entered in.
It was dark but no snow with an absence of wind.
They huddled together and all remained quiet
For they still did not know what the cave had inside it…

"I don't think we should be in here," moaned Freddy nervously.

"SSSHHHHH!!" whispered Thaddeus. "We may not be alone."

"Do you think there could be a mountain lion in here?" a nervous Becca asked.

"Or a bear?" Billy echoed.

"I don't like the dark," Steph whimpered.

"SSSHHHHH!!" Thaddeus again whispered. "I think we're o.k. If there is a bear in here it should be hibernating. If there is a mountain lion, I think we would have heard from it by now".

"This is a good time for everybody to brush off the snow and try to keep dry before we head out again," suggested Becca.

"Hey look!" Billy yelled. "There are some dried leaves, grass and branches. Maybe we could get a fire going and really warm up."

"Good idea!" everyone exclaimed.

The children all began to brush the leaves and grass into a pile.

"This is going to be a good campfire," an enthused Becca said. "Do we have any matches left?"

Everyone checked their pockets but to no avail.

"Well," Billy said. "Looks like Thaddeus is going to have to put his scout-training to work and rub a couple of sticks together."

"I think I'll try a couple of rocks first," said Thaddeus. "The grass is so dry that a couple of sparks could set it off."

All the children huddled around Thaddeus and the pile of leaves, branches and grass. It was kind of like 'dusk 'where the children were standing—a few feet in from the entrance and a few feet from where the cave really starts to get dark. A fire would provide some much needed warmth and add to some much diminished hope. Thaddeus explained to the group that the fire needed to be somewhat close to the entrance so there would be proper ventilation. A fire too far into the cave would be very dangerous if not properly vented. Carbon monoxide from the fire could be trapped in the air and cause drowsiness and eventual death. Thaddeus had learned this in the boy-scouts. And now the Boy Scout was chipping away at the rocks and successfully making some sparks. Becca held some brush near the rocks with hopes the sparks would ignite the grass and give them a ' torch ' to help make a bigger fire.

"Faster! Faster!" the children cheered.

"I'm trying! I'm trying!" yelled Thaddeus.

"It's going to work. It's GOT to work!" pleaded Stephie.

"I see some sparks! I see some sparks!!" roared Freddy.

Freddy was right. Thaddeus was able to cause some good-sized sparks when striking the rocks together. The sparks were dancing off the rocks and landing in the dry grass that Becca held.

"I see smoke. I see some smoke!" an excited Billy yelled. "And where there's smoke there is...."

"FIRE!!" Everyone cheered.

They had successfully kindled some of the brush Becca held. They had to carefully get it down to the pile of leaves without letting it go out. Real excitement was shown on the faces of the children. This was the first real warmth they had felt since leaving their schoolroom hours earlier.

"Enjoy it while it lasts," Thaddeus said with a red glow on his face.

"Well, it feels like a miracle now," Freddy said thankfully.

"Hey...look in the cave," Billy suggested. "You can see quite a ways in there."

"Gosh...I wonder how far it goes," Becca thought out loud.

"Wow! What if it went all the way through the hill," Freddy wondered. "It would save us a lot of walking."

"Sure. And what if…what if we got lost in the cave?" a nervous Stephie asked.

"Sounds risky to me, too," added Billy.

"It would sure make it easier to get home," said Freddy. "It will be a lot harder going up the hill this afternoon than it was coming down it this morning."

"Still sounds risky," said Billy.

"And scary!" said Steph. "We don't even know if that's the direction towards home."

"What if we do this," suggested Becca. "We make a torch out of this scarf and carry it into the tunnel. Now if the tunnel starts to go in different directions, we turn back immediately so we don't get lost. O.K.? But, there is a chance it might go straight through."

"Yea. And if the torch goes out at least we can feel our way back to here," Billy concluded.

"O.k." said Thaddeus. "But, let's make a couple extra torches out of some clothing. We'll bring them along and light them as we need them."

"Good idea," seemed to be the general consensus

"Save some of the larger branches that are in the fire, "Stephie suggested. "We can use them to make the torches."

"Right, Steph. And we can rip some strips off our clothing to wrap around the branches to make our torches," said Thaddeus.

Everyone was busy. All were scared. All were apprehensive. But, it was getting late and no one was excited about trudging through more snow. Thaddeus remembered the lesson about fire, caves and lack of ventilation. But, he believed the torch would just be big enough to see where they were going and they wouldn't use it long enough to cause problems. He reasoned that either they see a way out very quickly or they would head back to the entrance.

"All right, remember," reminded Becca. "One torch at a time. When it's about to go out we'll light another one."

"And stay close together. No stragglers," ordered Thaddeus.

They lit Becca's torch from the remaining fire and all looked toward the darkness ahead. Nobody wanted to take the first step. But, as soon as Becca started, they were right with her. The cave seemed to move through the mountain pretty straight. Once in a while it would veer left and than veer right. But, all in all—pretty straight. Without the torches, it would certainly be 'pitch black'. The group kept huddled closely and moved very cautiously.

"So far...so good," whispered Thaddeus.

"So far..." Billy chimed in.

They were lucky the tunnel didn't branch off in different directions. If that was the case they would head back quickly so as not to take a chance on really getting lost.

"I hope we are doing the right thing," Freddy murmured to himself.

No one really knew what the 'right thing 'to do, was.

"Nothing ventured...nothing gained." Becca said trying to lighten the gloom of the moment. "And at least it's a break from the bad weather."

They pressed on. When one torch was about to burn out, they would start another. Each torch lasted about five to seven minutes. They had used four and had four remaining.

“I think we can use two more torches,” responded Thaddeus. “We can travel much faster back than we have gone forward. We know what’s behind us.”

They all agreed to use two more torches and then head back to the entrance.

The group surged forward. Not too fast...but, fast enough for these young explorers. Time seemed to go by quickly as far as the torch was concerned. It seemed to be burning quicker than the previous ones.

“I sure hope we get some daylight soon,” Becca said. “We’re about one and a half torches from heading back.”

“Well. If nothing else we’ve found some shelter from the storm and can stay here until it blows over.” Thaddeus said for encouragement.

“Hold it!” Billy shouted as everyone stopped to listen. “Straight ahead... I saw two large eyes staring at us!”

Billy was even stuttering some in describing what he thought he had seen.

"Oh no," Stephie began to cry. "A lion or a bear...we're all going to be attacked!"

"Let's get out of here," Freddy pleaded. "Get that torch heading in the other direction!"

Chapter Seven

The group turned around. They were willing to let whatever belonged to the 'pair of eyes' to have that part of the cave. The class was heading back towards the entrance!

"Hold it!" shouted Thaddeus. "I saw them too. It's like they went around us and are in front of us again!"

The group huddled even closer together—if that was possible. There was only one pair of eyes visible now. The kids formed a 'body-of-one' with their eyes closed as tight as could be.

"I don't want to die," Billy kept repeating to himself.

"I want my mommy," Freddy cried.

All the kids joined in with 'choruses' of places or people they would rather be at or with. All of a sudden they heard a strange noise. It sounded like metal tapping on metal. It wasn't loud. It sounded like something muffled...like a bell without the "clang."

Everyone stopped shuddering and slowly turned to where they heard the strange sound. At that moment they heard the strike of a match and saw the flame light what looked to be the wick of a lantern. As the wick got brighter so did the lamp. And, for the first time in at least a half hour, the children could see everything.

What they saw was a complete and happy surprise. It was a little man holding the lantern. He was smaller than little. He was...he was...an...

"Elf! Look! He's an elf!" shouted Becca.

"The eyes belong to an elf!" Freddy chimed in.

The elf just stood and looked at the children. And the children stared at him with total exasperation. They had thought he was a lion or a bear. What a relief!!

"We are happy to see you," said Thaddeus.

"Can you talk?" asked Stephie

"Of course I can!" he replied. "I'm just trying to figure out if you are good kids or...BRATS."

"Brats... Not us!" Thaddeus assured him.

"We're lost and we want to go home," added Becca.

The others agreed with her.

"It looks like none of us are very happy then," said the Elf.

"Well, what's wrong with you?" asked Freddy.

The Elf proceeded...

Just look at me
Just look at me
so sad and full of misery
My bells won't ring
They work all wrong
They go "ging-ging"
when they should "gong-gong "
There's something wrong, something wrong
Please, can't you make the ging go gong?

The children responded…
What can we do? You look so sad.
But, trouble with bells we've never had.

The Elf countered...
Ever since a child your age
I've rung the bells to earn my wage
But lately it's that saddened ring
Instead of a "gong "it's always a "ging."

The kids…
What can we do to bring back the "gong "?
We haven't much time but we'll tag along.

The Elf
I'm not sure who has the answer
or even if we'll find a way
But, the bells lost their spirit

When I heard the words “hear it “
and in the sky I saw a sleigh.

Kids...
You looked in the sky and saw a sleigh?
But, Santa isn’t due today.

Elf...
That’s why I’m frightened.
It happened last year.
The sleigh goes ‘to and fro ‘
But the people stay here.

Kids...
If it’s not Santa
Then who can it be?
May we get a little closer
So it’s easier to see?

Elf...
Stay right where you are
I won’t be responsible.
No one dares
Not even the constable.
At first—even now
We all were quite curious
But, oh that poor man
He seemed so delirious.

'Stay away! Stay away!' he shouted from
a distance.
We've quarantined ourselves
with sadness our sickness.

Kids...
To quarantine...?

Elf...
Is to isolate till all the bad germs leave.

Kids...
But, with sadness their sickness...
How much longer must they grieve?

Elf...

None of us knows
If we do...no one tells
But, I still think their sadness
holds the mystery of the bells."

Kids...
You still think their sadness holds the mystery of
the bells?

Elf...
Yes. I still think their sadness holds the mystery of

the bells.

Freddy...

You still think their sadness holds the mystery of
the bells?

Elf...
Yes, I still.... Very funny you little moppet.
A cork in your mouth would suitably stop it!

The children all laughed.

Stephie...
I'm getting tired
And we're losing precious time.
Could we talk like normal people
And not make everything rhyme?

"Yes. Steph is right," said Thaddeus. "Time is flying by. We have to make a decision. Should we stay overnight in the cave or should we try to make it home?"

"Or should you follow me to a warm cabin that has a fireplace to dry your clothing," added the elf.

"And get something to eat?" Billy asked. "I mean I am really hungry!"

“We all are, “Becca interjected. “You’re not alone, Billy.”

Then the elf said, “Oh, I’m sure I could rustle up some grub... enough to feed you. We’ll have pancakes and waffles topped with berries that are blue.”

Kids...
 “It all sounds too good...to good to be true.”

Elf...
 Follow me
 you won’t need a ticket
 Here’s the end of the cave
 and the start of the thicket.

Chapter Eight

The kids were amazed at the difference in the weather. They had left a winter storm on one side of the mountain and walked into a winter wonderland on the other side.

“It’s beautiful,” Becca said with glee. “Everything is bathing in sunshine. What a difference a cave makes.”

“Oh yes,” said the elf. “It never rains and snows during the day on this side of the mountain. We hear it at night and see it in the morning.”

It was truly beautiful. Almost another world from what the kids had come through. However, their utmost thoughts were on warmth and dryness.

“We’ll be at my cabin soon,” said the elf.

“It’s very kind of you to help us,” said Stephie

“Oh, I’m happy to have company,” said the elf. “And hopefully, we can solve the mystery of the bells.”

"Excuse me sir," said Freddy. "We don't even know your name."

"Gosh. It's been so long since I've used it, "replied the elf. "I don't even know if I remember it."

"Oh come on. What is it?" asked the kids.

"It's Peculiar," answered the elf.

"What's peculiar?" the kids chimed.

"My name is Peculiar," responded the elf.

"What's so peculiar about your name?" the kids wanted to know.

"No! You don't understand." The elf explained. "My name…my name is…ok…are you ready? My name is Peculiar."

"Peculiar!" echoed the kids. "His name is Peculiar!!"

"I guess my parents thought it peculiar that I should be such a small baby when both my mom and dad were quite large," he said.

"Oh, that's the opposite of me," said Big Billy Tons. "My parents thought it was peculiar I was such a big baby when my mom and dad were quite tiny."

Everyone chuckled a little at Billy. He had a way of making everyone feel at ease. It was a nice feeling...having been so challenged by the day's events. These moments in the cave were the start of a positive bonding between the kids and Peculiar.

"Well, anyway. That's it. They named me Peculiar," said the elf.

"O.K...It's Peculiar," the children agreed.

The group of kids led by Peculiar was winding their way through the woods and up and down valleys until finally...

"There it is. There's my cabin," shouted Peculiar.

"All right!! I feel like we've found civilization," yelled Stephie.

And there it was. A fashionable cabin as fashionable as fashionable cabins are in this part of the woods. And practical. Very comfortable. Practical and comfortable. The kids were very happy. The immediate center of attraction was the robust fire in the fireplace. The group of lost Merrimenters immediately surrounded it

"Oh, the heat from the fire feels so wonderful. I didn't think I would ever warm up—let alone feel dry," said Becca in a cozy sort of way.

Nobody seemed to hear her. It had only been a few minutes...but, all the class seemed to be in a "snooze "pattern. They had all fallen asleep.

After a short period of preparation, Peculiar entered with pancakes, waffles, blueberries and hot chocolate.

"Everybody up! Everybody wake up!" Peculiar called out.

"Oh, wow! Warm food!" An excited Billy yelled.

The kids began cheering. Warm food—hot chocolate! Their feelings of despair had temporarily left them...hopefully, for good. They ate and ate and then found themselves snuggling by the fireplace again.

"I feel like taking a huge nap," said a yawning Freddy.

"I second that notion," echoed Billy.

"Wait a minute. We had a quick nap," a nervous Becca interjected. "Our parents are going to be worried sick if we don't get home or contact them."

"You're right," added Thaddeus.

"No sleeping for now," said Stephie.

"Not until we have a plan, anyway," said Thaddeus.

And then it was Peculiar's turn to say something.

> I opened my home to warm and feed you.
> That I have done. The best I can do.
> But, we made an agreement in the dark of the
> cave.
> Solve the mystery of the bells. Your promise you
> gave."

"He does have a point there," said Becca.

"Your right," added Stephie. "Without his help we might be frozen by now."

Everyone agreed.

"You said the mystery of the bells may be tied to the new people in the cabin and the sleigh that keeps going back and forth?" asked Thaddeus.

"Yes," responded Peculiar. "The bells started to 'ging' the very hour the sleigh first flew into the valley."

"Well then," asserted Becca. "I think it's time we head over to their cabin."

"What? I told you there might be an illness there!" a nervous Peculiar shouted.

"You said they were quarantined with 'sadness their sickness'," Billy reminded him.

"I see where you're going with this, Billy," said Freddy. "If we can make them happy, those 'gings' may turn into 'gongs'."

Everyone agreed. They would go up to the cabin and try to meet with the people who live there. With any luck, they might help make Peculiar's life a little easier and happier. After all, what good is a "bell-ringer" whose bells don't ring?"

Chapter Nine

The walk to the other side of this fascinating valley was very interesting. It was as if all the seasons of the year were next to each other like rooms in a house.

"It's like we are in the best of both worlds," an amazed Becca said.

"I know," said Freddy. "We have snow for sledding and skiing and yet, we can walk into an area that feels warm enough to go to the beach."

"What's with this place?" Billy asked Peculiar. "There are winters next to summers...snow next to sand...water next to ice...sunshine at one end of the valley and a blizzard at the other end. It's like everywhere we look there are different parts of different seasons. What's with this place?"

"Well, I have to admit it is a bit peculiar," admitted Peculiar. "How best can I explain it to you?

Peculiar is silent for a few moments of thought, and then says. "You know when the weather changes back at your village or how your parents talk about how it might change in the next day or two?"

"Oh sure. They do it all the time," answered Freddy. "Nice day. Do you think it will rain? How cold did it get last night? What's the wind-chill? It's not the temperature—it's the humidity. Cold fronts- hot fronts!! We hear it all the time."

The children were laughing and throwing in their own remarks related to weather conditions

"Well," said Peculiar. "Who do they usually give credit to for all the weather conditions?"

"MOTHER NATURE!!" the kids blurted out at the same time.

"And where do you think Mother Nature gets all her different weather conditions?" asked Peculiar.

A soft voice answered, "Here?"

"Yes!" Peculiar confirmed. "Welcome to Mother Nature's weather warehouse."

Peculiar went on to say, "If you want a heavy snowstorm just choose one over in the quadrant you kids accidentally wandered into. If you want searing heat or thunderstorms, you just have to go to another section of Mother Nature's weather warehouse."

"Unbelievable," the kids thought as their jaws hung down in disbelief. And, yet here they were. Maybe they were dreaming. Stephie pinched Billy's cheek to find out. "Ouch!" he yelped. "I guess we're not dreaming," Stephie apologized.

No, they weren't dreaming…the theatre of seasons was right before their very eyes. They started talking about all the fun they could have here. Like running from summer to winter the way their dads ran from a sauna to a snow bank.

"Wait a minute," Peculiar interrupted. "We still have a mystery to solve!"

"I know. But, I have to get out of this snowsuit for a while," said Big Billy Tons. "I'm roasting!"

It was like the 4th of July all of a sudden. HOT! HOT! HOT!

"Well, don't get too comfortable," warned Peculiar. "We still have some wintry conditions to go through before we get to the cabin."

Off they went. The group of people was winding up and down, in and out, over a long winding path. It was amazing to look back from the top of the hill and see the different scenes of weather co-existing in this 'Mother Nature's warehouse 'of weather.

"I wonder if we'll see Mother Nature?" an inquisitive Stephie asked.

"Yea…I wonder what she looks like," added Freddy.

All the kids started talking about how they thought Mother Nature looked.

"I bet she is beautiful," said Becca.

"She must be much bigger than me," said Billy. "How else could she move the different weather patterns around the world?"

"She must be strong," Thaddeus thought out loud.

"And fast," Stephie said.

It was Peculiars turn to speak.

"I doubt you will ever see her. But, you will feel her presence. Whenever she comes to the valley it seems like the waiting room at the doctor's office. All the different weather systems stop what they are doing and wait to see which one she will pick out to bring somewhere. It seems like a big arm sweeping in to take part of the weather system wherever she needs it leaving behind just enough of the system to grow in size until needed again."

"WOW!" the children cheered. "That's unbelievable!"

"I can't wait until she appears again," Freddy exclaimed.

"Well, you'll have to," said Peculiar. "We have business to attend to."

Chapter Ten

The children agreed and again the Merriment party was off over hill and dale.

At the top of the hill Peculiar raised his hand and signaled for the party to be quiet. He pointed ahead. The kids could see a cabin in the distance. There were puffs of smoke coming out of the chimney.

"Put your snowsuits back on," said Peculiar. "We are coming to another weather zone. It's the 'winter-in-Minnesota 'zone so it's plenty cold and windy."

"Burrr," shuddered Becca. "This will probably be as cold as an ice-box."

"Then add the 'wind-chill 'index to that ice-box," added Thaddeus.

"What is the 'wind-chill' index?" asked Stephie.

"Well, not only is the cold in a Minnesota winter measured by degrees," explained Thaddeus. "The 'wind-chill' factor is entered in. That is...how cold the wind is on your bare skin. This is calculated by using an equation that includes the temperature and how fast the wind is blowing against your skin. By this, they can determine how fast your skin would freeze if left uncovered for a certain amount of time. It can be very dangerous."

"Whew! It sounds very dangerous!" said Peculiar.

"Yes," said Becca. "You must be very careful to cover all your exposed skin on cold and windy days."

The kids were now suited up again and ready to move into the 'winter-in-Minnesota 'zone. It was a quiet winter setting. Peculiar motioned for them to slowly sneak up by the windows in order to see what was happening inside the cabin. As they approached the windows they could see a little old man and a little old woman sitting at a table and apparently working on some toys. The toys didn't appear to be new toys. The toys had scratches, tears, dents and bumps and looked like they had been saved from the dumps. The couple at the table physically resembled Mr. and Mrs. Santa Claus. As the kids quietly whispered they compared the style of clothing to the Clauses. Everything appeared the same except for the color. Instead of a bright red suit with white trim, these two had bright green outfits with white trim.

“They look like Mr. and Mrs. Santa Claus,” a stunned Stephie said.

“SSHHH,” cautioned Peculiar.

“No beard,” whispered Freddy.

“SSHHH,” an even louder Peculiar stressed.

“But, they do look like Mr. and Mrs. Santa Claus,” Big Billy agreed.

‘SSSHHHHHHH,” an exasperated Peculiar warned.

At that moment, the elderly couple heard the commotion and raced toward the voices. The children saw them coming and ducked below the window out of sight.

“That’s funny,” said the old man. “I thought I heard children’s voices.”

“I’m sure you did,” the lady said. “I heard them too.”

“I miss the company of children,” the old man said fondly.

“Oh, what fun we use to have with them,” said the lady as she opened the window.

“Wouldn’t that cheer us up, Mrs. Claus,” said the man. “If we could be in the company of children again?”

"It sure would be nice," answered Mrs. Claus. "In fact...I have a whole new batch of cookies made."

"And some hot chocolate?" an excited Billy Tons said as he jumped up.

"Get back here," ordered Peculiar.

"Enough hot chocolate for everyone," responded Mrs. Claus.

"Cookies and cocoa sound good to me," said a smiling Becca.

"You'll be sorry," warned Peculiar.

By now everyone was standing and in view of the couple with the last name of Claus.

"Oh, come in children," implored Mrs. Claus. "We would love to have some company."

The children did not have to be asked twice. They were headed to and through the door of the cabin.

Peculiar was a little skeptical. "That's not what you said when you first arrived here. You told us to stay away because you were quarantined."

"Yes," Mrs. Claus agreed. "Quarantined with sadness our sickness."

"We feel happier now," added Mr. Claus. "We found a way to bring happiness back into the world."

"Yes," said Mrs. Claus. "We repair toys that no one would think repairable."

"We find them in places where people no longer have to look at them," explained Mr. Claus.

"In dumps…garbage cans…you name it," added Mrs. C. "And the funny thing is…with some effort. We can make them almost new again."

"And get them to children who may not receive anything for the holidays," Mr. C said.

"Seems like I've read about someone else doing the very same thing," suggested Freddy.

"Oh, that's true," responded Mr. Claus. "But, that's another story."

Everyone laughed.

"And we have a system to make new packaging to put the toys in so no one can tell the toys had been used before," said Mrs. Claus. "Everything looks brand new."

"Wow!" Thaddeus exclaimed. "It looks like a toy store in here!"

The children were excited to look at all the toys. Some were in the middle of repair. Some were all repaired and waiting for their packaging. And, some were all packaged and waiting for final holiday wrapping.

"It's like we are in the middle of a dream," Stephie said in a daze.

"Yea…I don't know if I want to wake up," added Billy.

"This is no dream," said Mr. Claus as he put platters of cookies on the table for the children to enjoy. "When we first arrived here it might have been like a bad dream."

"Repairing those toys has been good therapy for us," added Mrs. Claus.

"I'm confused," Peculiar interjected. "We didn't know what to expect when we approached your cabin. We didn't know who you were or what had happened to you. We certainly didn't expect as pleasant a setting as this."

All the children agreed. The hot chocolate and cookies were disappearing quickly. Between the treats and toys it was a feast for the eyes and stomachs.

"You are right, Mr. Peculiar," said Mrs. C. "It wasn't real pleasant then. But, enough about us—let's hear about you."

Chapter Eleven

The children introduced themselves. Then Thaddeus went on to tell Mr. and Mrs. "C" how these children from the town of Merriment had arrived at this " toy-repair shop " in the middle of Mother Nature's valley. He said he almost had to pinch himself to make sure he wasn't dreaming. What he and his schoolmates had gone through so far today would make anybody think they were in a dream. Thaddeus told them about the search for a special tree to put in the courtyard. He told them how they had encountered some nasty weather conditions, lost their dog and had left their teacher behind in order to get back home for some help.

"We forgot all about Miss Dubbin!!" shrieked Becca

"We have to rescue her!" yelled Stephie

"We need to look for her now," added Freddy.

"Was she very far from the cave I found you in?" asked Peculiar.

"Not far," Billy answered. "We had trudged through the snow for about an hour after we left her."

"Yes," added Thaddeus. "And we were moving pretty slowly through the snow."

"Are they talking about the cave that separates the blizzard section from the serene section, Mr. Peculiar?" asked Mrs. C.

"Yes, they are," answered an embarrassed Peculiar. He had never been called "Mister" before.

"Well Sam. You could send the sleigh to look for her," suggested Mrs. C.

"Sleigh? Say, who are you two anyway?" asked Becca with a puzzled look on her face.

"Oh, I'm sorry," said Mrs. Claus. "You told us your name but we never told you ours. We are Mr. and Mrs. Samuel Claus."

The kids looked at each other in amazement.

"Samuel?" asked Thaddeus. "Is that formal for Santa?"

"No. It's formal for Sammy," said Mr. Claus. "I am Sammy Claus. Brother of the more famous Santa Claus."

The kids all responded at once: "WHAT!" "I DON'T UNDERSTAND!" "YOU HAVE GOT TO BE KIDDING!" "SOMEBODY WAKE ME!" "I DIDN'T KNOW SANTA HAD A BROTHER!" "SAMMY CLAUS???" "WAIT TILL I TELL THEM BACK HOME!!" "I CAN'T WAIT FOR 'SHOW AND TELL '"

"Yes, children," Sammy said. "I've been around as long as brother 'S '... as I like to call him."

"Brother 'S '," a bemused Becca said.

"Yes, Brother S and I go 'way back '…as you well know," said Sammy.

"Well, how come we have never heard of you?" Freddy asked.

"We were always behind the scenes," answered Mrs. Claus or 'Mrs. C. 'as Sammy liked to call her. "We chose a less-hectic lifestyle."

"We were in charge of recovering the toys that the children did not want," said Sammy.

"When kids received gifts they didn't like…"
"Or had two or three of the same toy," added Mrs. C.
"The toy would be rejected," continued Sammy. "And sit in the corner of the toy closet never knowing the love of a happy child."

"Sam was in charge of the T.R.R. Association," said a proud Mrs. C.

"The T. R. WHAT?" a confused Peculiar asked.

"The Toy Recovery and Recycle Association," she explained. "Sammy would send a few of the elves out days after Brother S…"

"Santa," Stephie confirmed.

"Yes," said Mrs. C. "After brother Santa had delivered the toys."

"It didn't take long for the elves to find the unwanted toys," said Sammy. "Loneliness can put a gloom over the whole home. Each of the toys wanted to be the perfect gift for the kids. But, unfortunately, some weren't. The toys would feel so unwanted and lonely that the elves would rescue them and bring them back."

"How would they find them?" asked Freddy.

"Well," said Sammy. "When a toy is lonely it will have a certain aura or glow to it. While not visible to the human eye, we can see it with the use of our 'A.D.' "

"Your what?" pleaded Peculiar.

"Our Aura Detector," answered Sammy. "It can detect whatever mood a toy or person is in."

"So you just fly over the roofs of homes and stores and when you detect a lonely toy with your... A.D... you find a way to rescue it and bring it back to the North Pole," summarized Peculiar.

"Precisely," Sammy answered with a big smile. "And there we change it or fix it so that the next year it has a better chance of a warm reception wherever it goes."

"I'm starting to feel a little guilty about a few of my toys," Becca said sadly.

"Yes. And I just thought some of mine had been lost," added Billy. "I guess I didn't care enough to look for them."

"You wouldn't have found them," said Mrs. C. "There are so many children in the world who appreciate receiving these toys that we put them into our 'Pass It On 'program."

"Wow! Are we learning some things today," an excited Freddy said.

"The 'Pass It On 'program," said Becca. "What a great idea."

"Wait a minute, everybody!" yelled Stephie. "We are forgetting about Miss Dubbin."

"That's right!!" yelled Peculiar along with everyone else.

"Oh yes," said Sammy. "Miss Dubbin…your teacher. I have an idea."

"What is it, Sam?" asked Mrs. C.

"We'll send the 'A.D. 'with the sleigh to find her," Said Mister Claus.

"Use the Aura Detector to find her?" asked Stephie.

"Sure," said Sammy. "She has to be giving off some sort of aura. Whatever it is, the A.D. will find her and bring her back. Let's go program the sleigh now so it will search in the approximate area you left her in."

“Can we ride along?” asked Thaddeus.

“No,” Sammy went on to explain. “The sleigh will make better time by itself. When the A.D. finds her, the sleigh will settle down next to her, play her a tape-recorded message assuring her that everything is ‘ A OK ‘ and then bring her back.”

“Yeah! Yeah! Yeah! “The children screamed excitedly.

Sammy, Peculiar and the kids went out to the sleigh and added the A.D. along with plenty of blankets, some food and water. After programming the sleigh and the A.D., the group sent it on its way. The sleigh was quick to reach a high altitude and head in the direction of the ‘blizzard’ section.

“I sure hope it’s not too late, “said Freddy.

“Oh, she should be o.k.,” a hopeful Thaddeus said. “It’s been about four hours since we left her.”

“I just hope she hasn’t given up on us,” said Freddy.

“Let’s stay positive and let the A.D. do its thing,” suggested Becca.

"Becca's right," said Sammy. "Let's go in the cabin and give it a little time."

Chapter Twelve

The group headed into the cottage and proceeded to have some apples and hot chocolate.

"I'm sure glad we were able to meet you children," said Mrs. C. "And you too, Mr. Peculiar."

"Well, I feel much better having met you also," answered Peculiar.

"While we're waiting for Miss Dubbin," asked Stephie. "Do you think we could help fix some of the toys?"
"Sure you could," said Sammy. "You could start by washing some of them. Many of the toys don't need repair...just a good clean-up and a new package."

Without hesitation, the children were into the toys. They did whatever was needed to make them new again. What a production line. It got to the point where the toy would start with Sammy and by the time it got to Stephie at the end of the line, it was packaged, wrapped and ready to go. Time went by quickly.

"This is wonderful," said Mrs. C. "We are way ahead of schedule."

"Whew!" said Becca with a big sigh. "This has been work. But, I feel so good knowing we are doing something nice for someone else."

"I feel real good about this too," added Billy.

"Say Sammy," Freddy said. "May I ask you a question?"

"You sure can, Freddy," answered Sammy.

"Your brother Santa," said Freddy. "Has a bright red suit and a long white beard."

"Yes," said Sammy.

"You have a green suit and no beard at all," Freddy continued. "Any particular reason?"

Sammy C. became very quiet. He couldn't look anybody straight in the eye. He went to the window and gazed out over the valley very despondently. The silence was deafening. No one spoke for a moment or two until Mrs. Claus finally said…" I guess you children and Mr. Peculiar deserve an explanation. For as long as I can remember, Samuel was more involved with his brother's distribution of toys than most people know."

"Oh, honey," Sammy said with a tear in his eye. "These people don't want to hear this sad story."

"Please," said Becca. "Please let her finish."
The children nodded in agreement. She went on..." Everyone knows what an awesome job it must be to deliver all the toys in one night. Santa had to have the finest sleigh powered by the finest deer following the best directions for that evenings run."

"Best directions," Sammy interrupted sadly. "What a job I did."

"It wasn't your fault," insisted Mrs. Claus.

"What happened?" implored Peculiar.

"Yes...what happened?' the children wanted to know.

"Well, Sammy was always in charge of laying out a map of directions for Santa to follow in order to have the smoothest night of delivery," she said. "If he was to run into some bad weather he would know about it and make the necessary adjustments."

"You mean like fly around or above the bad weather," added Thaddeus.

"Precisely," Mrs. C said. "By following Sammy's directions, Santa could avoid certain areas and go back later."

"There has got to be more," Freddy assumed.

"Well, it seems…" Mrs. C went on. "It seems that over the decades, every few years the weather has almost flip-flopped from what it normally is for that time of year."

"The Kid," murmured Sammy.

"The Kid?" echoed Stephie

Mrs. C continued. "Yes, the Kid I'm sorry to say. It seems that every two to seven years this century the weather does things we could not imagine. When Sammy would tell Santa an area would be snow-filled, Santa would arrive there and be in the middle of a rainstorm."

"The Kid," Sammy murmured.

"And in the areas where it's usually warm, they might be having their first snow-storm," she said.

"The Kid," murmured Sammy.

"So you see," added Mrs. Claus. "All the weather systems seem to do a "flip-flop" around the world...and you never know when it's going to happen."

"That's why we came to this valley," said Sammy. "We needed to find some answers."

"Everyone at the North Pole started to blame Samuel," said Mrs. C. "They thought he was trying to undermine Santa. Can you imagine that...his own brother?"

"Well, Santa didn't feel that way," added Sammy.

"I know," agreed Mrs. C. "But, try to convince some of the citizens of the N.P."

"N.P.?" questioned Freddy.

"North Pole," answered Peculiar.

"And then those stubborn North Poleans," Mrs. C said bitterly. "They insisted that Samuel shave off his beard so as not to be mistaken for his brother."

"Well, Santa didn't agree with that either," added Sammy.

"I know," she said. "But, you complied with their silly wish."

"You seem to like my clean-shaven face when we do a little cuddling, my dear," said Sammy with a twinkle in his eye.

"Oh Samuel!" Mrs. C blushed. "You stop that kind of talk in front of the children!"

The children giggled and laughed and laughed and giggled. It seemed to cheer up Sammy too.

Mrs. Claus cleared her throat loudly to stop the chortling.
"I must insist the room and those in it quiet down so I may continue with my explanation."

The room and those in it quieted down quite quickly.

"Anyway," Mrs. C went on. "We weren't too popular there and decided to come here and try to find out from Mother Nature if she had anything to do with the strange weather patterns."

“The Kids,” said Sammy. “That’s who Mother Nature thought were at fault.”

“The Kids!” the children all yelled with shock and surprise.

“Oh, not you kids,” Sammy assured them.

“Every time Mother Nature thought she had everything back to normal something would go wrong again” Said Mrs. C. “And, if it wasn’t the kid who caused it, it was his sister or alter-ego or whatever.”

“Mostly the kid, though,” said Sammy. “According to Mother Nature…sometimes two years would go by without anything out of the usual happening.”

“Maybe even seven or ten years,” added Mrs. C.

“But then, here he would come again,” interjected Sammy. “Stealing weather patterns from Mother Nature’s valley and messing them up all over the world.”

“The Kid?” Becca said quizzically.

“The Kid?” Thaddeus thought.

"El Nino!" Freddy, Stephie and Big Billy yelled all together.

"El Nino!" responded Thaddeus and Becca with a shout.

"El Nino?" Sammy and Mrs. Sammy asked.

"Yes," said Thaddeus. "The Kid is El Nino."
A very puzzled Sam says, "The Kid is El Nino?"

"We've studied him in school," Becca said. "El Nino is the name given to a part of the Pacific Ocean that warms up when the West blowing trade-winds settle over the Pacific along the equator. The sun-warmed water that usually heads towards Southeast Asia ends up heading back towards the Americas."

Thaddeus continued. "Moist air warmed by the warm water below it, rises high into the sky and forms storm clouds. The weather kind of goes crazy around the world because the 'jet-streams' are affected by this different heating of the atmosphere."

"Crazy is a good word for it," Billy added. "Where it should be cold…it's warm."

"Where it's normally dry…it's wet and stormy," Stephie said.

"Sounds like the world gets turned upside down," Sammy concluded.

The children agreed. They told the Claus's about people playing golf in Minnesota in the middle of the winter while people in southern vacation states were fighting storms and flooding.

"That explains Mother Nature," Sammy said. "She kept mumbling about 'the Kid 'and how she needed a vacation after she straightened everything out."

"SSHHH," Mrs. C said as she pointed to the sky. "Listen..."

Just then you could hear the sleigh returning to the cabin. Everyone ran out to greet the sleigh and hopefully...Miss Dubbin

"I can't wait to see her!" yelled Big Billy

"I hope she's ok." Stephie yelled.

Chapter Thirteen

All the kids were yelling with excitement as the sleigh made its way to the landing. And sure enough…it had found her AND the tree and brought them back.

Everyone spoke at once: "Miss Dubbin….."

"Are you ok?"
"How is your ankle?"
"Are you cold?"
"Are you hungry?"
"Can you walk?"
"Could you believe that sleigh?"
"Can you believe this place?"
"The tree! She remembered the tree!"

Miss Dubbin had a big smile on her face. It was a smile that communicated how happy she was to have been rescued and how happy she was to see her class looking safe and well taken care of.

"I feel like I'm dreaming," Miss Dubbin said. "I had almost given up hope of any rescue. I'm so happy..."

Her voice trailed off and tears came to her eyes. Everyone became somewhat emotional. Those 'tears of joy 'led to a big 'group-hug '. This lasted for a few moments. When they started to separate, smiles came back to everyone's faces. The group was together again.

"So tell me," Miss Dubbin said with a broad smile on her face. "Where are we? How did you get here? Who are these kind people and how can I buy one of those sleighs?"

Everyone laughed.

Becca introduced Miss Dubbin to Mr. and Mrs. Samuel Claus and to Mr. Peculiar.

"What a pleasure to meet you Mr. and Mrs. Claus and you Mr. Peculiar," said Miss Dubbin.

"We've heard so much about you, Miss Dubbin," Mrs. Claus said.

"Yes," Sammy said. "You were a very brave woman to stay behind knowing the children would make better time without you and your bad ankle. How bad is your ankle?"

"At first, I thought I might have broken it," responded Miss Dubbin. "That's why I insisted the children go on alone. I didn't want to hold them back. The day was going too fast and they needed to find some shelter."

"Yes…we found a real 'peculiar' shelter," Freddy said.

The children giggled and Peculiar smiled at his new friends.

"Sam," Mrs. C suggested. "Let's go inside and warm some food for Miss Dubbin. We'll have a party!"

"Yes! Party time! Let's have a party!" the kids responded.

The 'party' headed for the cabin while the kids began to tell Miss Dubbin about the past few hours.

Thaddeus began to tell her about their trip through the cave, their chance meeting with Mr. Peculiar and their journey to Sammy and Mrs. Claus's cabin. Stephie told her about Mr. and Mrs. Claus, the toys, and the sleigh. Big Billy told her about the great pancakes and muffins Mrs. C. made for them. Freddie told her about the reason for Sammy and Mrs. Claus being there in the first place and Becca went on to tell her about Mother Nature's warehouse.

"You know, boys and girls," Miss Dubbin remarked. "I've always heard of Mother Nature but I never knew there was an actual 'weather warehouse'. This is just amazing."

"Well, I suppose the weather has to come from some place," offered Freddie.

"I suppose it does," Miss Dubbin agreed.

At that moment the dinner bell began ringing.

"The dinner bell is ringing!!!" shouted Freddie. "Did you hear it, Mr. Peculiar? Did you hear it?"

"Well, it's nice to know that somebody's bells will ring," responded Mr. Peculiar.

"Well, try yours," suggested Becca.

"Oh, what's the use?" a depressed Peculiar said. "They haven't rung in ages."

"Try them! Try them!" the children yelled. "Try them!"

Mr. Peculiar looked at the bells he had tied around his waist and said, "Well, if it will get you kids to quiet down…I'll try them. "

He slowly began to rub the bells very lightly as if he was warming them up for the big test. And then he did it. He bent forward a little bit so the bells would hang away from his body. He began to 'slap' the bells in a manner he had not done for quite some time. And guess what? No more "gings". The bells worked! The children screamed with laughter and no one was happier than Mr. Peculiar. He started to dance and the children followed him. They danced around the sleigh, around Miss Dubbin and right up to the front door of Sammy's cabin.

"Now, that's a sound we haven't heard in a long time," a smiling Sammy said.

"Yes. The laughter of children and the ringing of bells," Mrs. Claus agreed. "They sound wonderful."

Mr. Peculiar was so happy. He stopped playing the bells…looked at the children, Miss Dubbin, the Clauses and proclaimed, "The quarantine is over! Happy days are here again!!"

"They sure are," said Sammy as he hugged Mrs. Claus and gave her a big smack on the lips.

"It's nice to have friends again!!"

The children all laughed and cheered while an embarrassed Mrs. Claus said, "Samuel Claus! You behave yourself. Everybody...time to eat!"

A very happy group of people entered the cabin and gathered around the table.

"I insist that our most recent guest, Miss Dubbin, sit at the head of the table," Sammy said.

Miss Dubbin was honored to do so.

"We've been so busy telling you about our adventures, Miss Dubbin," said Becca. "That we haven't given you a chance to speak."

"Yes, tell us about your experiences after we left," an eager Stephie said.

"It must have been scary," Freddy added.

Miss Dubbin began to tell them about her time spent alone in the woods. Everyone was very quiet as they listened intently to every word she spoke.

"My heart was so heavy as I saw you disappear into the storm," Miss Dubbin related. "I felt so guilty for letting us get into that situation."

"But, nobody knew what we were getting into," a sympathetic Thaddeus said.

"I know," Miss Dubbin said. "But, I have to take responsibility. I should have taken a map and chartered out our course ahead of time."

"Well, I picked the part of the woods I wanted to go into," said Becca. "And you…being the newest resident of our village, thought I knew what I was doing. I guess I was kind of trying to show off."

"Well, we all are to blame," said Big Billy. "None of us were familiar with that part of the woods but we all were too proud to admit it."

"He's right, you know," said Freddy. "We were wrong to pretend we knew our way. It endangered the whole group."

"Well, you're here now," interjected Mrs. Claus. "And that's what is important"

"And how lucky we are," added Stephie. "This has been one heck of a day!"

Chapter Fourteen

Sammy could notice Miss Dubbin wince in pain when she would have to put some weight on her ankle. He asked her, "How is your ankle feeling now, Miss Dubbin?"

"I think it's getting better all the time," a brave Miss Dubbin replied. "Luckily, I had remembered some of my old first aid training having to do with sprained ankles in order to keep the swelling down. I alternated wrapping it in snow for a few minutes and then wrapping my scarf around it to keep it from freezing. I repeated that process quite a few times while trying to keep the rest of my body warm by constantly staying active.

"What a frightful time you had, my dear woman," said a sympathetic Mrs. Claus.

"I must admit," Miss Dubbin said. "When that sled landed and I heard the message giving me instructions,

I wondered if I was hallucinating. AND, if I was hallucinating...please, no one wake me up!!"

"Oh, you're not hallucinating, Miss Dubbin," said Peculiar. "Welcome to Mother Nature's Weather Warehouse."

"Thank you, Mr. Peculiar," Miss Dubbin said gratefully. "The children were telling me about this 'theatre of seasons '."

"And now," said Thaddeus. You can understand how we did get lost so easily. No one is to blame. The weather changed too often for us to know what direction we were going."

"I suppose you're right," conceded Miss Dubbin. "But, I don't know if your parents will believe us."

"PARENTS!!" yelled Stephie. "We've forgotten all about our parents!!"

"Your right, "Becca added. "I bet they are getting real nervous about now."

"Yes," an excited Freddy said. "They were expecting us back hours ago."

"You know, Sam," suggested Mrs. Claus. "I bet there's a certain sleigh that could whisk them back in no time."

"You're right, Mrs. C.," responded Sammy.

"Wow!" shouted Freddie. "A ride in the sleigh! This will be great!"

The other children were just as excited. Soon they would be home with their parents and pets. But as fast as they got excited, they soon became a bit somber.

"What's wrong?" asked Mr. Peculiar.

"Well," Said Billy with his chin lowered." I think we just realized that as happy as we are to be going home safely, we're sad to be leaving our new friends,"

"We really like it here, too," voiced Becca

Everyone nodded in agreement.

"Well, you just might have to come back for a visit," countered Mrs. C.

Shouts of happiness were in the air as the children agreed it would be a good idea to make a return visit.

"Yes," Sammy added. "Maybe you could lead the next 4th grade class here while searching for that perfect tree."

"Great idea," shouted Freddy.

"Just listen for the bells," said Peculiar as he played a little 'riff 'on them. "I'll lead you the rest of the way."

"All right, children," said Sammy. "Gather up all your coats, hats, scarves, boots, knap-sacks and whatever else and let's head to the sleigh."

"Don't forget to take something to snack on," said Mrs. Claus. "I'll pack a big sack of lefse for you."

"Lefse?" Billy Tons asked.

"It's flat as a pan-cake and made out of potatoes and flour," responded Sammy. "It's my favorite. You put butter on it—some people like sugar. Then you roll it up and eat it."

"Well," said Billy thoughtfully. "I normally don't like to eat food but I'll make this one exception just to try it."

Everybody laughed heartily.

"Here we go then," said Sammy.

“We can’t leave without a ‘group hug’,” Stephie insisted. “We may not see Mrs. C and Mr. Peculiar for quite some time.”

Everybody agreed and gathered in one circle with Mrs. C. and Mr. Peculiar in the middle. The circle moved together with hugs and pats on the backs and promises of seeing each other again. It was sad. Everyone thoroughly enjoyed each other’s company.

“I bet you’ll be seeing a lot of Peculiar,” Becca said to Mr. and Mrs. Claus.

“I sure hope so,” responded Mrs. C.

“Those are words I like to hear,” Peculiar said feeling the warmth of friendship. “In fact, I plan on staying here with Mrs. Claus until Sammy gets back.”

“And I thank you for that,” Sammy said.

In the last few hours there had been bonds of friendship developed between the class, the Clauses and one fellow named Peculiar.

“We better be on our way,” Miss Dubbin hinted.

The whole party was dressed warm and headed for the sleigh.

Chapter Fifteen

“Everybody pile in,” ordered Sammy.

What excitement! The kids all found a spot to sit and eagerly awaited their departure.

Everybody had a puzzled look on his or her face as if something was missing. Then suddenly at the very exact moment they shouted. “THE TREE!!” “THE TREE!!” “WE CAN’T FORGET THE TREE!!”

Peculiar brought it over to the sleigh. It didn’t look like a typical Christmas tree anymore—hardly any needles on it—many of the branches were broken or missing. It was in pretty bad shape.

“Why don’t I just fly us over to the forest and we’ll pick out a fresh full new tree,” suggested Sammy.

“OH NO!!” “NEVER” “NO, NO, NO,” shouted the children.

“This will be the only tree for us,” insisted Thaddeus with the complete approval of the class.

“This tree saved our lives,” stated Stephie.

“More than once,” added Freddy.

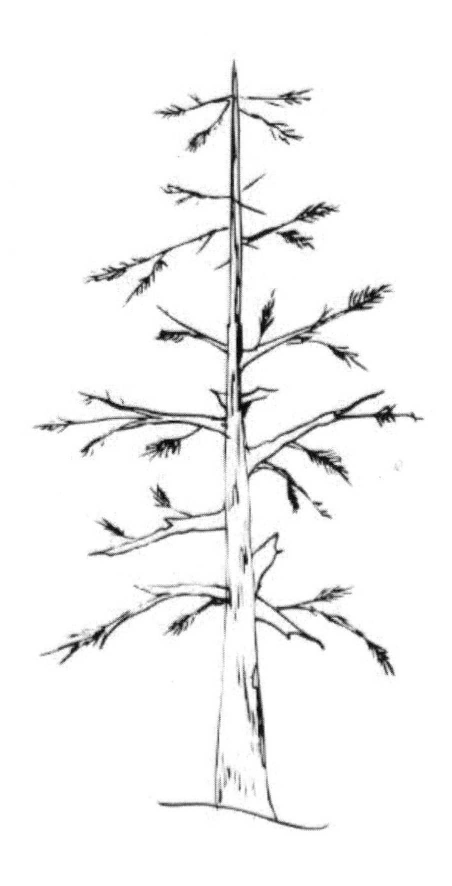

"OK. I get the picture," said Sammy. "Bring it on board and find a nice place for it."

"There you go," says Peculiar as he handed the tree up to the kids. "That should be just about everything."

"Have a great trip," Mrs. Claus tells the sleigh party.

"See you soon," a hopeful Peculiar adds.

"Bye-bye," all the children respond. "Take care of yourselves! Thank you so very much!! Bye!!"

"Oh, Mr. Claus," said Mrs. Claus caringly. "I expect you back safe, sound and soon."

"Safe, sound and soon," repeated Sammy. "Safe, sound and soon"

The sleigh began to lift off. The children, Miss Dubbin and Sammy waved to Peculiar and Mrs. C. down below.

"I took the 'automatic pilot 'off so we could do a little sight-seeing on our way back to Merriment," said Sammy.

"We would love to," was the general reaction of the passengers.

Sammy pulled back on the controls as the sleigh ascended high into the sky. What a ride this was turning out to be. Everyone held on and loved the rush of wind in their faces as the sleigh climbed and cut through the atmosphere like nothing they could ever imagine. There were screams of excitement much like you would hear on a fast Ferris wheel or roller coaster.

“Maybe we could take a little more time to get home,” a nervous Miss Dubbin suggested.

“I received your message loud and clear,” a grinning Sammy Claus said. “I’ll back it off a little.”

“I see reins…but no reindeer,” remarked Freddy.

“Well, I didn’t want to take away from my brother’s image,” said Sammy. “People expect to see him with reindeer. I came up with a different means of propelling my own sleigh.”

“How does that work?” asked Thaddeus.

“Well…to make it as simple as possible,” answered Sammy. “In the compartments just below us I have certain apparatus that take in more air from the front of the sled than can be contained within the sled.

Therefore, it is forced out the back of the sled and provides us with proper propulsion."

"Proper propulsion," stated Becca. "Sounds simple enough to me."

"Oh sure," the children and Miss Dubbin laughed.

"Well children," said Miss Dubbin. "However this sleigh works, it's a pleasure to be properly propelled."

"Right on!" yelled Freddy. "This is unbelievable!"

"Hold on," Sammy yelled. "I'll fly you high enough over the warehouse to see all the different weather systems."

It was SPECTACULAR!!! The sleigh was high enough to see miles and miles of different 'weather fronts'. It seemed to go on and on. They could see what almost appeared to be different 'rooms' of weather. They saw hailstorms, rainstorms and snowstorms next to torrid heat and tropical summer. There was warm and wet followed by all kinds of sunshine. Every conceivable type of weather was before their very eyes!!

"I'm not even going to attempt to tell anybody about this," declared Miss Dubbin.

"Unbelievable...unbelievable," the words just trailed off everyone's lips as they were completely mesmerized by this awesome panoramic view.

"She sure is amazing, isn't she?" asked Sammy.

"Mother Nature's Weather Warehouse," mumbled an amazed Billy Tons. "Who would have 'thunk it'?"

"Wow, wow, wow," is all a completely awe-struck Stephie could say.

"Sammy," Freddy inquired. "With all the different choices of weather in the warehouse, how come you chose the cold winter section to stay in?"

"Well, Freddy, my good man," answered Sammy. "Image has something to do with it. You never have imagined the Claus family sitting on a beach in a tropical climate, have you?"

"No, I guess not," replied Freddy.

"We feel pretty comfortable in the winter setting," Sammy went on. "Besides, Mrs. Claus loves to have that fireplace roaring as she 'cooks up a storm '...mmmm wait. Bad choice of words...as she displays her culinary abilities in the kitchen."

Everyone laughed.
Sammy went on. "But, I'll let you in on a little secret. Every so often I do change the weather pattern over our cabin. I bring over a few hot days of summer and Mrs. Claus and I get out the lawn chairs and sit back and bask in the sun. It's very relaxing and it seems to help my depression.

"Well...there are studies that relate depression to a lack of sunshine," said Becca.

"Yes," added Freddy. "Some people need to have a special light in their home to combat depression caused by a lack of sunshine."

"Well, it sure seemed to help my disposition," said Sammy. "And when I felt better, I'm sure Mrs. C. felt better."

"She is quite a woman," Miss Dubbin stated.

"Quite a woman in deed," agreed Sammy. "I remember the first time we tried that sunbathing stuff. I got burned to a crisp. I was as bright red as a tomato. If I had had my beard, you would have thought I was Santa. Mrs. C. laughed and laughed. "Me sitting there in almost nothing but my 'birthday suit' looking like my famous brother."

"That must have been a sight to behold," commented Stephie with a grin on her face as the rest of the children were giggling. "And if it makes you feel better…why not keep it warm the whole year round?"

"Image, I suppose," said Sam. "Isn't that silly? Letting ourselves remain depressed knowing that the sunshine could cheer us up. Good old 'image'."

"Many people are like that," said Miss Dubbin. "Always worried about their peer-group and their image."

"Yes," said Becca. "Just like we were kind of worried about our 4th grade image measuring up to Thaddeus's 5th grade image."

"I didn't know I had one," Thaddeus said with a surprised look on his face."

"For sure," said Becca. "That's one of the reasons I started us off in the direction I did when this whole adventure began."

"Not to mention the fact that we wanted to prove that the girls were just as smart as the boys," commented Stephie.

"Well, you never had to prove anything to me," said Thaddeus. "I've known you all my life."

"Nor me," offered Big Billy. "We've always known we are smarter…JUST KIDDING!!"

They knew he was kidding.

"Yea," added Freddy. "You two are cool and cool. It's been a pleasure being lost with you."

Everyone agreed and laughed. The class had never felt closer as a group --as actual friends. This adventure had opened everyone's awareness of the other people sharing their space—their strengths and their weaknesses.

"They call this 'bonding'," said Miss Dubbin.

"Then 'bonding' it is!" yelled Freddy.

"Bonding forever," the kids cheered.

"And blankets forever," a chilly Miss Dubbin shuddered. "Do we have anymore blankets?"

"Blankets! We have blankets!" sang out Sammy. "Check under your seat. We have all the blankets you need."

With that, he pulled back on the controls and the sleigh heartily climbed even higher into the sky. They were so high by now that they could see the horizon as it curved with the shape of the earth. Then, with almost the same suddenness as their take-off, Sammy slowed the sleigh to a complete stop.

"Oh man," said Billy. "It's like we're on the Ferris wheel when it comes to a quick stop at the very top!"

"But, it's not swinging and I don't feel scared," an amazed Freddy said.

"That's because we're not attached to the earth like a Ferris wheel is," explained Sammy. "We are suspended in mid-air with no attachments."

What a picture this was...a sleigh full of passengers 'sitting on top of the world' as the old song says. Everything was so quiet... so crisp...so inspiring.

"This is just awesome!" an overwhelmed Billy stated.

"A monumental occasion," said the usually calm Thaddeus. "It's so vast...so impressive!"

"And so unbelievable," an amazed Stephie stated.

"If you look real hard," Sammy observed. "You can just barely see Merriment."

"I see it! I see Merriment!" yelled Freddy.

"I do too," chimed in Billy.

"Where? Where is it?" asked Thaddeus. "I don't see it!"

"Must be your older eyes," kidded Freddy with laughter in his voice. "Your vision is starting to go."

“Just a minute there, Frederick Rodriguez,” said an amused Miss Dubbin. “My ‘older eyes’ can see it just perfectly. And I think I see your father waiting for you with a big scowl on his face.”

“Oh no,” said Becca. “We’re having such a good time we keep forgetting to go home.”

“We better head on in,” Miss Dubbin said to Sammy.

“Then Merriment it is,” a resolute Sammy Claus said.

Chapter Sixteen

The sled was off. The smiles were on. What an adventure...racing on the jet streams across the sky. Who would believe their story? Who could they share this incredible story with? Who had time to think of that now? Enjoy the moment! Whew! What a moment!!

"You will have to let me know where you should be dropped off," said Sammy. "I had better not be seen."

"Why not?" asked Stephie.

"Some of the towns-people may be related to the North Poleons," answered Sammy.

"So?" asked Billy.

"So they might think that Sammy was responsible for some of Santa's misfortune with the bad weather," explained Thaddeus.

"But, it was 'The Kid !' "Countered Freddy.

"Yes! It was El Nino!" a most agreeable Stephie said.

"El Nino or not," said Miss Dubbin. "People have very strong feelings about things that upset their life-styles. We had better pretend like we are coming out of the woods when we get there...perhaps from behind the blacksmith's shop."

"Yes," agreed Becca. "I think I can lead us home from behind the blacksmith's shop."

Everyone had a good laugh over that statement.

Sammy guided the sleigh behind the 'tree-line' around the village. In a few moments he was gently resting the sleigh behind the shop Miss Dubbin had suggested. It was almost dark now. What a long but short day it had been. And now a moment had arrived that no one looked forward to...the sad good-byes. Stephie already had a few tears glistening over her cold rosy cheeks.

"I'm going to miss you so much," she said.

Everyone felt the very same...even the two adults—Sammy and Miss Dubbin. It was amazing that such a strong feeling of friendship could develop within such a short period of time.

Chapter Seventeen

All of a sudden there was a JOLT of voices in the air coming out of the woods and from the other side of the blacksmiths. “There he is! Grab him! Grab the reins! Get the kids out of here! Now we’ve got you! You won’t get away!”

The kids were shocked and frightened. What was going on? These were their parents acting like a ‘crazed ‘mob.

The towns-folk had Sammy in their grasp. The whole scene was frightful. People grabbing at Sammy, the sleigh and hardly noticing their children were safely back home.

“Stop it! Stop it!” yelled Miss Dubbin.

The children joined in. “Stop it! Stop it! Why are you doing this? He’s our friend.”

"Now we know the rumors are true," said a townsman. "There is a crazed Santa 'wannabe' in our midst." All of his fellow Merrimenters agreed.

"No! No!" yelled Freddy. "He saved our lives." All of HIS fellow Merrimenters agreed with him.

"He tried to ruin Santa's deliveries by making it rain," yelled a townswoman. "Our Christmas was almost ruined!" All of HER Merrimenters agreed.

"He didn't do that," yelled Becca. "El Nino did that." All of HER fellow Merrimenters agreed.

Now…if only everyone could agree with everyone else in Sammy's favor. It was not to be.

"Bring him to the town square! "Someone yelled. "He kidnapped our children!"

"KIDNAPPED! ARE YOU CRAZY?" yelled Thaddeus.

"Now, young man…don't interfere," instructed Thaddeus's father.

"But, dad…you've got it all wrong," insisted Thaddeus. "He saved our lives!"

"Well, we'll see about that," answered his dad.

"Enough talking," someone yelled. "Let's take him down to the town square!"

"Yes!" another yelled. "Bring him down for everyone to see!"

Everyone was in agreement. Everyone, that is, who hadn't been on the sleigh. And speaking of the sleigh—Becca whispered to Freddy, "Do you think you could sneak over by the sleigh during all this commotion and program it to head back to Mrs. Claus and Peculiar to let them know what has happened?'

"Consider it done," answered Freddy.

As the towns-people headed in one direction, Freddy headed in the opposite direction…toward the sled. With all the fuss over Sammy, nobody noticed Freddy talking to the sled. In a few moments the sleigh was a streak in the sky.

The gatherings of people were now assembled in the heart of Merriment…the town square.

The mayor was the first to speak. "You never liked wearing that green suit, did you?"

"I never disliked it," answered Sammy. "It actually served a purpose."

"And what was that?" the mayor asked.

"Well, as everyone knows," stated Sammy. "My brother and I are almost identical twins...when I had my beard anyway. With the green suit, people could tell us apart easier."

"But, you were envious, I bet," guessed the mayor.

"You might say I was green with envy," laughed Sammy.

All the children laughed along with Miss Dubbin. The towns-folk weren't as amused.

"No, I wasn't envious." Sammy went on. "It served a purpose. I like green and if Santa wanted to be in pink with orange polka dots, I couldn't care less. Next question please."

"Toy delivery," said Becca's mother.

"Yes?" responded Sammy.

"There have been times over the years when many of the children didn't receive their toys from Santa for days after Christmas," an irate mother said.

"And the way we hear it," another parent went on to say. "Is that you purposely confused him with the directions to our homes so that he would run into rain and mud and not get here in time."

"It was El Nino!" The children insisted.

"They are quite right, you know," added Sammy. "When I charted out the map for my brother on Christmas Eve, all the weather systems were analyzed and the routes were thoughtfully laid out."

"Then what happened?" Freddy's dad asked.

"El Nino!" the children yelled.

"The Kid," Sammy responded.

"The Kid?" the townspeople asked.

"Yes," persisted Stephie. "El Nino is the kid. And he's the one who messed up Santa's deliveries."

"How?" asked Billy's father.

“I was hoping we wouldn’t have to get into this,” a reluctant Miss Dubbin said.

Miss Dubbin, with the help of the children, went on to explain to the townsfolk all about Mother Nature’s Weather Warehouse and how El Nino, with the help of his sister, La Nina, would move un-natural weather systems to different parts of the world surprising the citizens of that particular region.

“And at the same time,” added Sammy. “Confusing Santa and his reindeer.”

“Please believe us,” pleaded Big Billy. “We’ve been there and have seen it with our own eyes.”

“Mother Nature’s Weather Warehouse,” the older Tons stated. “That’s incredible!”

Just then a whirl of noise and movement could be heard and seen above the town of Merriment. Everyone paused to look up.

“It’s the sleigh!” yelled Stephie. “You did it, Freddy! You did it!”

Chapter Eighteen

All the children and Miss Dubbin were excited. The towns-folk were confused. A couple more circles around the village square and it gently landed on the ground. The first person off the sleigh was a very perturbed Mrs. Claus.

"What have you done with my husband?" she said with authority. "If you have done any harm to him you will deal with the wrath of Mrs. Samuel M. Claus!"

The townspeople were abuzz. "Mrs. Claus in our village," whispered Stephie's mother. "There are so many recipes I want to get from her."

"Here I am, honey," yelled Sammy.

The townspeople parted to show Sammy in the middle of the crowd. Mrs. Claus went to him immediately.

"Are you o.k. my sweet love?" she asked.

"I'm fine," he said. "We were just having a long over-due discussion."

The town-folk all nodded their heads in agreement. Just then they heard a loud sound as if someone was 'clearing' their throat.

"HHHMMMMMM, HHHMMMMMM," was the sound.

Everyone turned and looked to see a tiny but statuesque person emerging from the sleigh.

"And who might this person be?" Asked the mayor.

"Permit me to introduce myself," the small man said. "My name is Peculiar."

"Peculiar?" the townsfolk responded.

"Here we go again," was the thought and look on each of the children's faces.

"Yes, my name is Peculiar," he said.

"What is so peculiar about it," asked Stephanie's confused mother.

"People," insisted Miss Dubbin. "Listen carefully. He's telling you his name. His name is...are you ready?" She spelled it out. "P E C U L I A R! Peculiar. Get it?"

"Peculiar. Yes, his name is Peculiar," said the Mayor. "What do you think we are? A bunch of village idiots?"

"No Mayor," said Thaddeus. "We just wanted to save you the time it took us to figure it out."

"Very good then," a satisfied Mayor said.

"HHMMM! HHHMMMMM!" was heard from an impatient Peculiar. "Could I have your attention, please? I am here to represent my defendant...one Samuel M. Claus."

"What does the M. stand for," a curious Stephie asked Mrs. Claus.

"Oh," she whispered with a sly grin. "It stands for 'muffin'. He's my precious muffin."

Stephie was almost sorry she asked.

"Go on, Mr. Peculiar," said the Mayor. "What do you have to say for the defendant?"

The children all circled around Mr. Peculiar and whispered in his ear everything that had been discussed thus far. Frankly, he was happy for that. It was taking all his acting ability to keep this pompous attorney image going.

"People of this hearing," Peculiar stated. "My fellow practitioners of the law have brilliantly filled you in with a total explanation of the ware-house, the kid, and the confusion that followed concerning Santa's deliveries. Now permit me to introduce to you three well-known and distinguished 'colleagues of the holidays' to testify as to the character of one Mr. Samuel M. Claus."

As Peculiar was speaking he made a grand gesture to the sleigh and at that moment a small figure threw off a blanket and stepped out. He walked toward the crowd.

"Witness number one," Peculiar said with pure enjoyment. "This young fellow was to be part of a Christmas concert but almost had to withdraw because someone had broken his drum. The defendant heard about the situation and immediately came to the rescue to help fix the drum. And now, little drummer boy...could you point out to the fine people of this town exactly who it was that fixed your drum in time?"

Without hesitation, the drummer boy smiled and pointed straight at one Samuel M. Claus. The people were silent for a moment. And then someone yelled out… "Look at his whiskers! They seem to have popped out a bit! "

Sammy rubbed his whiskers and seemed to notice they were a bit stubbier than before. He hadn't had a beard in months.

"So he fixed a drum," Mr. Tons said. "What does that prove?"

"If I could have your attention again, kind folks," an impressive Mr. Peculiar said passionately.

And a figure began to walk toward the people. It was a giant snowman who told of a very warm winter when he melted down to nothing. Sammy had kept the coals that were his eyes and kept the carrot that was his nose and kept the stones that formed his mouth. The next winter Sammy made sure this snowman received all these vital parts so he could continue on as a normal snowman.

"Could you please point in the direction of the person who helped you through this critical situation?" asked Peculiar.

The snowman smiled and pointed at one Mr. Samuel M. Claus. And again, there came a silence—almost an embarrassed silence if you can imagine such a thing.

"Look at his beard!" someone yelled. "It's growing again!"

Sure enough...it was growing again. It seemed to grow whenever someone testified to the good character of Sammy M. Claus. Sammy was enjoying this. He certainly missed and loved his beard.

"And now, for my last star witness," the honorable Mr. Peculiar stated proudly.

As he turned to the sleigh the last cover was thrown off the mystery guest. A large robust figure walked toward the crowd. There was no doubt who this was.

"Santa! It's Santa!" Stephie's little brother yelled out. "Santa! Santa! Santa!!"

It was Santa...wow! Everyone went crazy to have such a celebrity in their midst. Santa Claus...everyone was so happy he was here in Merriment. But, the happiest in this whole gathering seemed to be Santa himself.

"Brother!" Santa yelled out as he made a dash towards Sammy. "How I've missed you!"

"And I've missed you," a sincere Sammy responded.

The two brothers embraced each other.

"I had no idea where you had gone," said Santa. "Everyone I asked could only say you left in a hurry with no forwarding address."

"I felt it was best for everyone if I stepped out of the picture," explained Sammy. "I started to believe that maybe I was guilty of misjudging the weather systems and in turn messing up your delivery route."

"Nonsense!" snapped Santa. "That is utter nonsense!"

People had never seen Santa in any degree of anger.

"Blaming my brother for something he had no knowledge or control of is imbecilic," protested Santa. "It was the Kid and his Sister who had been messing with the weather patterns!"

"Thanks, brother," said Sammy. "The children knew of the "Kids ". They call them El Nino and La Nina."

"You mean this whole case against your brother, Sammy Claus, is truly a result of El Nino and La Nina?" asked the Mayor.

"That's right," answered Santa as he pointed proudly at Sammy. "My brother has never been anything but a positive force in the production and delivery of gifts every Christmas. Without him on my team I had even given thought to retiring."

The Merrimenters were aghast to hear such a statement. Just then someone yelled…

"Look! His beard! It's almost as long as Santas."

"It is as long as Santas!" someone else yelled.

Wowee! There they were. The two Claus brothers arm in arm looking like identical twins except for the colors of their suits. Sammy always preferred green, if you remember. Everyone was laughing and celebrating. The general consensus was that Sammy was completely innocent of any wrongdoing when it came to weather patterns and Santa's routes.

Mrs. Claus picked up Mr. Peculiar and gave him a big smack on the lips. "Beet-red "might best describe his complexion after that experience.

Everyone joined in a circle around the children, Mrs. Claus, Miss Dubbin and Mr. Peculiar. They in turn formed a circle around the two Claus brothers. Everyone was cheering and dancing.

In the midst of all the celebrating, Stephie and Freddy slipped out. Something was missing. The reason for all the adventures that had happened that day was nowhere to be seen. We are talking about---the TREE. No matter how raggedy or worn that tree looked, it was definitely going to take its place in the middle of towns-square.

"Excuse us! Excuse us!" yelled Freddy and Stephie as they entered the circles of celebrators with the tree in hand. "I think we have forgotten something."

Immediately, the tree was put in place...downtown Merriment...town square Merriment. You wouldn't think It much of a sight—until you heard the story. Then you realize that this tree was a true hero for the help it supplied when needed. Everyone was very proud to honor this tree at this time.
And then, the surprise of all surprises...Scooter appeared. From around the back of the now famous blacksmith shop, the little mascot who started the adventure with the group this morning came running

with a face full of snow and excitement in his bark. You can imagine the excitement his appearance caused with the kids.

"Scooter! Scooter!" they shouted as they ran to greet their friend. He was just as excited to see them. They took turns hugging him and brought him to the middle of the circle and danced with him around the tree.

The celebrating continued...continued until everyone began to tire. The party began to slow down a bit—not in spirit—just in physical weariness. It had been a long day. Everyone kind of collapsed where they were and just stared at the tree. It was a nice quiet moment shared by everyone.

Chapter Nineteen

Then Billy had a thought. "Do you remember Sammy, when you mentioned switching weather patterns at your cabin just to enjoy a bit of summer for a change?"

"I remember, Billy," answered Sammy.

"Well, how did you actually get the weather pattern to move over your cabin?" Billy asked.

"Easy," said Sammy. "I put up a wall of lasers all around the weather system."

"So, it's boxed in?" Billy asked.

"That is correct," said Sammy. "When it's locked in with the lasers it follows wherever the source of the lasers leads it."

"Wow," said Freddy. "That must be some laser gun."

"And it sits right on the sleigh and leads the "boxed in weather" to wherever we want it," added Sammy. "When we bring in the new pattern, the old pattern just moves aside."

"That's incredible," said Thaddeus. "It seems so simple and yet so unbelievable."

"Incredible is right," added Becca while holding Scooter in her arms. "Who would believe any of this day without being a part of it?"

"One thing about that laser gun," interjected Santa. "We have kept it a secret from Mother Nature. She has her own methods of moving weather systems. I don't know which is better…hers or ours. But, we prefer ours."

"Well, I was thinking," Billy pondered out loud. "If you can move weather systems around…why couldn't you move a cold weather system over El Nino when needed and a warm system over La Nina when needed?"

"I never thought of it," replied Sammy. "I guess it never occurred to us because of the distance and also not knowing that we could remedy the Niño's by doing it."

The young fellow might be on to something here," stated Santa.

"Yes indeed," replied Sammy. "Done correctly, we could put the normal weather patterns back where they belong."

It's worth a try, Samuel," stated Mrs. Claus.

"It is indeed worth a try, Mrs. Claus, "replied Sammy.

"Brother…I'm going to let you handle these 'Nino' children," said Santa. "I'm needed back at the 'Pole'. As soon as you're finished though, I could use your help back home."

"I'd like nothing better than to return to my old position," Sammy answered proudly.

Mrs. Claus had a broad smile on her face. She was so happy that the two brothers were back together again as a team. Just like old times.

Then Santa added "Course, I'll need a ride back to my sleigh, Mr. Peculiar."

"Oh sure, Mr. Claus," replied Peculiar. "I think we can drop you off at your sleigh on the way to Mother Nature's Warehouse. Right Sammy?"

"No problem," Sammy answered. "But, what do you mean 'we '?"

"Well, I just thought you might need a co-pilot," answered Peculiar.

"I think he needs six co-pilots," suggested Becca.

"Now you're talking," was the general attitude of the adventurous Merriment kids.

"Well, I don't know," was Sammy's thought spoken out loud.

"Samuel, I think you should leave it up to the parents," suggested Mrs. Claus.

"Yes, yes, yes…" cheered the children as they ran to their respective parents. "Please mom…please dad…can we? Huh? Please let us!!!"

And of course the parents had different thoughts about the whole situation.

“I don’t know,” one replied. “It could be dangerous.”

“You just got home,” another said.

“What about your homework?” added one more.

All the voices working together sounded like a chant.

“Please mommy, please”
“But you just got home”
“Please daddy, please”
“This is no time to roam”
“Please let us go”
“Is your homework done?”
“One time, please”
“Life’s not always fun”
“Oh please, mommy, please”
“What does your father say?”
“Oh please mommy, please”?
“ HE SAID IT WAS OK???!!”
“Oh please daddy, please”
“What does your mother say?”
“Oh please daddy, please”
“SHE SAID IT WAS OK???!!”
“ OK…OK…OK”
“OK…OK…OK”

The kids were off running toward the sleigh while the parents pointed fingers at each other thinking the other had OK'd everything. Eventually everyone was seated in the sleigh--- Sammy, Santa, Mrs. Claus, Thaddeus, Becca, Freddy, Stephie, Billy and Mr. Peculiar.

"Another adventure of a life-time," yelled Freddy.

And of course, everyone responded with the same enthusiasm.

"I wouldn't worry," Mrs. Claus cautioned the townsfolk. "Sammy is a very careful person. If there is any danger he will turn right back. Right, Sammy?"

"For sure, Mrs. C.," yelled Sammy.

"OK then," shouted Santa. "First stop…my sled. Then I'll take your Mrs. Claus back to your cabin and I'll head back to the 'Pole' to give the citizens the good news of your return."

"Wonderful," exclaimed a happy Sammy. "Everybody ready?"

They were.

"Then, we're off!!" Sammy bellowed.

And off they were!! What a sight to see. The sleigh headed up and off toward the horizon. Though the parents were worried for their children, they were soon caught up in the excitement of it all. Can you imagine what this whole day must have been like? If they didn't know any better they might have felt they were part of a children's story.

The sleigh was now approaching where Santa had left his sleigh to ride with Peculiar.

"I'll see you very soon," said Santa to his brother Sam as he began to climb into his sleigh. "We have a lot of work to do between now and Christmas eve. I hope you're up to it."

"I can't wait to get back to see my old friends and be a part of the merriest time of the year," an excited Sammy Claus said to his brother as he helped his wife into the sleigh next to Santa. And, as he gave his wife a wink, Sammy said to her, "I'll see you even sooner my little sweet baby-cake".

"Yes, Samuel," replied Mrs. C. "I'll pack a picnic basket for our trip to the 'Pole'. And children...I expect to see you real soon, too. Don't be strangers. And the same to you, Mr. Peculiar." And with that she gave Sammy a smooch. The children giggled.

"Bye, bye," all the children yelled. "We'll miss you. See you soon! Bye Santa. Good-bye!"

And then the sleighs parted. It was time to go to work.

Chapter Twenty

"I forgot to give Santa my 'wish-list'", Freddy remembered.

"Oh, don't worry," said Sammy. "Leave it in the sleigh and I'll make sure he gets it."

All of a sudden there were five children scurrying for writing materials in order to submit their wish lists to Santa.

"Mother Nature's Weather Warehouse straight ahead," Sammy shouted into the star-lit night.

And with that, he headed in the direction of the coldest winter room he could find.

"If we are going to cool down Mr. El Nino," Sammy said. "We might as well find a good cold blizzard to dump on him."

The sleigh was just about there. The children could tell because the blankets seemed lighter and thinner than before. It was getting real cold.

“Bundle up,” yelled Sammy. “I’m about to start the ‘laser-strategy’. “

And with that he started to aim the laser gun from the sleigh to a far corner of the “blizzard” room. He moved the laser up and down until it formed one big wall of laser light. Then he moved to the next corner of the “blizzard” room and began the process all over again. Twice more and the “blizzard” room was all encapsulated in this laser box of beams.

“Wow! Is that ever neat!” yelled Stephie.

“And pretty,” a duly impressed Billy Tons remarked. “The colors are just beautiful!”

Everyone agreed. Imagine an area about the size of a small city all contained in one big beautiful box. And, imagine that box flying through the air. WHAT A SIGHT!!!

“OK “, said Sammy. “So far… so good. Now we have to move this weather system over 'the kid' and release it. Six or eight loads like this dumped on the ocean above 'the kid' might make him a little less disagreeable."

"Samuel Claus," a shivering Peculiar said. "You are an absolute genius."

Everyone agreed with the little "bell-ringing defense attorney" as the sleigh headed out over the ocean to find the under-water lair of the 'kids'. It wasn't long before Sammy had the "aura-detector "turned on.

"I see you have the 'A.D.' on," observed Becca.

"Yes," said Sammy. "This will show us the aura of the ocean and where its hot-spot is."

"The hot-spot being El Nino," Thaddeus commented.

"You are correct," said Sammy.

Given the size of this ornery hot spot, it wasn't long before they found it. The sleigh moved to right above this part of the ocean.

"When I shut down the laser gun all the laser walls will disappear," said Sammy. " When that happens, the blizzard should hover over this spot for a while until gravity takes over and settles all these arctic conditions right down into the ' brat '."

If the children had paid as much attention to their schoolwork as they had to this long day's adventure, they would be the smartest of scholars. They were completely absorbed in this never-before tried method of removing one Mr. El Nino and one Ms. La Nina.

"There it goes," yelled Sammy. "One mid-winter blizzard compliments of the citizens of Merriment."

The children all cheered. This was a historical undertaking. Even if it didn't work, what an experience they had been part of.

"That's once, you little brat," shouted Freddy at the swirling El Nino. "How many more trips do you think it will take, Sammy?"

"Well, I hate to say this," said Sammy. "But, with everyone on this sleigh, I'm afraid we're carrying too much weight. And for that reason, we aren't able to pull as large of a weather system as we need. I might even use smaller cubes and pull four or five at a time."

"I think I know what's coming next," said Billy.

"I think you're right," agreed Becca.

Everyone knew that Sammy had a job to do and if they weren't in the sled he could get the job done sooner and then get back to the North Pole to help his brother.

"We understand, "Thaddeus stated. "We should be able to watch you against the night sky from Merriment."

"That's right, "agreed Freddy. "Do you have any fluorescent colors?"

"Yes," added Billy. "We can watch those boxes glowing in the dark as they pass over us."

It was agreed then. Sammy would take the children back to Merriment and he and Peculiar would continue on with their mission.

In a short period of time the sleigh was again hovering over the town of Merriment. The children could see their parents waiting for them standing around the pride of the Merriment town-square—the highly thought of—the reason for the whole day of incredible adventures and wonderful memories--- the Merriment Town-Square Christmas Tree. It wasn't the fullest most beautiful tree in the world. But, there wasn't another tree on the whole planet more loved than this one.

The children, Sammy and Peculiar knew there was no need for more words. The bond between these people would never be forgotten. Someday they would meet again. They all knew that.

The sleigh touched down and the party of children departed to the cheers of their townsfolk. A wave and a few tears and the sleigh was off again. And for now...the young Merriment residents were proud and happy to stand next to their fellow Merrimenters and bathe in the thoughts of the past day as they watched beautiful and bright colossal boxes pass over their village.

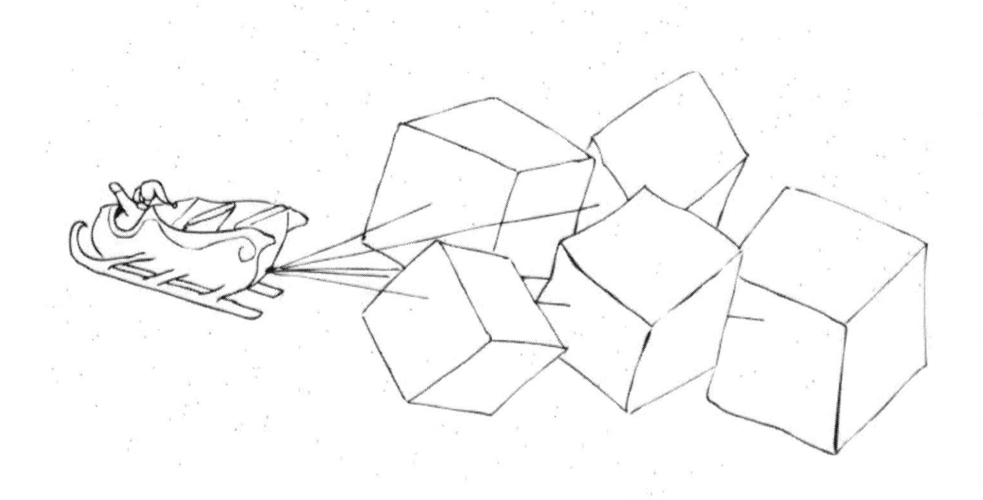